WHITEOUT

A DARK LEOPARDS MC - SOUTH TEXAS NOVELLA

R.R. BORN

To Kris Shade Riley
I would have never guessed when I gave you a book that it would have led me here.
Thank you for supporting Indie and New Authors and thank you for stopping at my table.
You're a rare treasure.

CHAPTER ONE

The torrential rains turned a refreshing motorcycle ride into something cold and nasty, then into something white and fluffy. Oz pulled over to a bar in the middle of nowhere when the snow flurries distorted his view of the highway. He knew better than anyone that Texans didn't know how to drive on ice or anything resembling frozen precipitation. He parked his silver and black Fatboy motorcycle near the corner of the bar, away from the crowd of snow-covered cycles.

Oz Zhang had always been a loner, but he found a family with the Dark Leopards Motorcycle Club. Something weird had been going on with him the last couple of months. He wanted to think it was only wanderlust, but his mother, rest her soul, told him this day would come. The day when a snow leopard had to come in from the cold.

As the Dark Leopard's clubhouse filled with mates, it was difficult to be around all the love and pheromones. Now, that his president, Six, had found his mate, Twistie, there hadn't been any kind of peace in the clubhouse. They had no concept of quiet sex. He didn't begrudge his brothers and sisters for finding love. Even seeing the club's Sergeant at Arms - Fina, and her damned warlock mate kissing filled him with a spurt of jealousy and he didn't like it. The long bike rides had helped him release some of the anger and most of the resentment, but he wasn't quite sure anything would really help.

Oz banged out a quick text to Six to let him know the weather situation and that he'd get back to San Antonio when he could. The last sign he saw clearly was Italy, Texas, a few miles back. He wasn't sure what town he'd actually stopped in.

Six texted a response in under a minute: Stay safe, my brother.

A lion shifter in black military fatigues partially blocked the front door of the bar.

Of course, I'd find the one lion's den bar in the middle of nowhere.

Oz squeezed past him, and motioned to pull off his leather duster, then the strong stench of more than lions hit him. The place was filled with scents of bear and wolf shifters among other things, along with the smell of humans. The last thing he wanted was for any of them to see his Dark Leopard's cut, his leather club vest. He turned to leave, but he couldn't even see the bikes he'd just walk past to enter this hole in the wall. There was no need to go back out there.

Melted ice dripped off his long coat as he walked in. No one looked his way. The small bar looked to be standing room only and the country music playing could be barely heard over the cacophony of voices. He squeezed through the crowd, getting a growl here and a hiss there, but nothing fight-worthy as he worked his way to the bar.

There were two bartenders working, but the female bartender's movements were as fluid and graceful as a cat.

When one of the drunken patrons reached for her, she eased out of his way. There was something intriguing about her. Oz stood at the end of the bar and watched her work. She flipped a tequila bottle in the air, then filled a line of shot glasses. A giggle rolled up in him when she twirled the bottle opener like a baton through her fingers before opening three long neck bottles of beer. Oz schooled his face, covering his mouth with his hand, after realizing he was still smiling. Plus, no self-respecting leopard *giggled*.

This was the first time Oz questioned himself as to if he had a type. Everything about this woman checked the '*my kind of woman*' box in his mind. She stood about five-eight or five-nine, with beautiful dark-skin and dark eyes. Even the faux-hawk fade with blonde highlights on her natural hair flipped a switch for him.

When she moved to his end of the bar, he looked away.

"Hey, what can I get you?"

Oz blinked, then looked her way, then around him to make sure she was talking to him.

"Yeah, you," the female bartender said with a smile. "What can I get you?"

Her raspy voice made his cock stand at attention. He moved closer to the bar so that no one else could see what this woman was doing to him. He opened his mouth, but nothing came out. It had been a long time since he'd held a conversation out loud. His tongue felt heavy in his mouth and dry as a desert.

"I'll come back if you're not ready." She turned to leave.

"No." With his quick cat-like reflexes, he touched her hand to stop her. He cleared his throat and tried again. "Please. Wait." The moment he touched her, a frisson of recognition surged through him.

Mine.

She didn't snatch her hand away, nor did she haul off and slap him. Which, if he was being honest with himself, he kind of expected both. "I'm sorry. I know you're busy." He reluctantly released her hand.

"No. It's okay. What can I get you?"

"Whiskey sour," he said and when she turned to leave. "And I really didn't mean—" He lifted his offending hand.

She came back and wrapped her hand around his upheld one with a smile. The warmth from their first touch was nothing compared to the lava racing through his veins now. Her unusual scent surrounded him as she leaned in to speak. In that moment, it felt like they were the only people in the room.

"I know," she said, then winked before she walked away.

Oz took a deep breath; he needed to smell her again, but instead he got a nostril full of cigarette stench, then hints of weed invaded his senses, along with gun and motor oil. Finally, buried under all of that, a light citrusy scent... her scent. It slammed into him, hitting him so hard he stumbled. There was no doubt, this woman was his mate... and she was wholly human.

It wasn't unheard of; he just didn't expect a human to be the person to complete him. He wanted to know more about her and couldn't help it. He used his telepathic powers to try and read her mind.

Crash.

The bartender staggered, blinking furiously while shaking her head surrounded by broken glass and spilled whiskey.

Did he do that to her? He couldn't connect into her mind. There was only distorted snow, like when a TV station loses its signal.

"What the fuck, Ronnie? You know that's coming outta

yo pay," the greasy, long-haired bartender said before slamming down two long necks.

She cut her eyes upward with a slight lip curl. "Yeah, Boss."

"Now, clean that shit up." He stepped right through the middle of the mess as he walked by.

"Where's my drink?"

"Clumsy bitch."

The barrage of insults continued as Ronnie tried to clean up the mess. "Okay, guys. I'm coming," she said breathlessly.

For fuck's sake, his woman, Ronnie, was on her knees cleaning up for these bastards and all they could do was talk bad about her. Without thinking, he jumped over the bar in one graceful leap. That one move made all the belligerent bastards near the bar stop yelling. He pulled the tall trash can closer to his woman and lowered to her level, clasped her hands gently, and took each glass piece from her.

Ronnie smiled wistfully. "Thank you."

Already, he knew, he would do anything to see her smile. He smiled back, then used the small hand broom and pan he found nearby to clean up the rest.

"Hey!"

Oz lifted his eyes towards Ronnie's boss.

"Get the fuck from back here!"

Ronnie looked between the two men, then whispered, "Maybe you should go." She touched his arm and gave it a little squeeze. "I really do appreciate the help though."

His heart started to thump in double time. This woman, his woman, was trying to protect him and she didn't even know him. No one had tried to protect him in a long time. He patted her hand with a smile before he stood and positioned himself between the guy and her. His leopard's fur tingled just under his skin. It wanted complete control, but Oz couldn't do that in a room filled with humans and other shifters. It would be a complete bloodbath. He released the cat just enough to get his point across. From one blink to the next, his eyes went from pale green to a deep emerald.

The guy took a step back. "Ronnie, tell your boyfriend to get from back here or that'll be your job!"

Ronnie said from behind him, "Thank you, but you probably should go."

When he didn't respond, she touched his hand and moved into his line of view. The cat had yielded his threat when she touched him.

"Your eyes—"

He lifted his brows in response, but Ronnie didn't seem phased, she just kept talking.

"My sister's eyes do that sometimes. Change colors. When she's angry, mostly. I wish mine would, then dumbasses would know not to touch me." Ronnie looked around at the few guys still at the bar. "Everything's okay now. Let me get you your drink."

Her brown eyes were beautiful to him. If he continued to look at her, he could get lost in them. His leopard dialed it down, and he emitted a pained grumble that didn't sound remotely like, "Thanks."

She laughed and turned him around by the shoulders. "You know the way out." But before kicking him out, she leaned in and kissed him on the cheek, then gave him a big push.

The crowd made kissy noises, but Oz didn't care. Ronnie didn't know that that kiss had just sealed her fate.

THE BACK CORNER had one stool near the small riser. In

some circles, it could be called a stage, but truthfully it was a five by five area with a step. Just enough room for one singer, and maybe a guitarist. The stool was hard as a brick, but he laid his back against the wall to have a full view of the front door, the two exits and Ronnie. No matter the place, Oz hated having his back exposed. If someone wanted to attack him, he was damn well going to see them coming.

The cigarette and cigar smoke gave the place a hazy glare. It also assaulted his sense of smell, but not enough to make him leave. When he was younger, a crowded place like this would have sent his telepathic ability into overdrive. In those days, the overstimulation would have made him pass out, but now he had full control over his ability. If he wanted to hear one person's thoughts or multiple, he could. Occasionally, with a clear mind and deep concentration, he could detect a person's deepest/darkest secrets - even if they weren't thinking about it.

A petite girl who looked barely old enough to come into this type of establishment, let alone work there, placed a tall glass, complete with a cherry, in front of him. "She must really like you."

"Who?" Oz whispered.

"My sister." She looked back at the bar. "She never gives anybody *anything*, and that, my friend, is on the house."

He reached into his pocket and pulled out a wad of bills, thumbed off a twenty, then placed it on the table. The girl stepped back.

"I was given strict instructions not to take any money from you." She used one finger to push his money away. "But I'll give you a tip." She looked around, then leaned in and whispered into his ear.

He couldn't concentrate on what she was saying, because he caught a whiff of something that smelled like home and unfamiliar at the same time. The deliciously sweet scent reminded him of fresh-baked apple pie. He inhaled again, and this time the aroma stunned him. There was no way Ronnie and this girl were sisters. Ronnie was human, and this girl was about to go through the *Sí-sheng Shu*.

The first change and heat.

This girl was a shifter.

CHAPTER TWO

W hat was going on with her? She let this guy touch her? Ronnie never let anyone lay a hand on her. There was something about him though. It was the way he looked at her with those cat-like green eyes. Nothing like the other yahoos in this dump. She knew exactly what they wanted. This guy looked at her like he wanted to eat her up. That should scare her, but it didn't.

When he touched her, electricity seemed to hum up and down her spine. It was like he'd completed something in her she didn't even realize was missing. She wanted more of that.

Yep, and people in hell want ice-water, Ronnie, she said to herself as she made the next drink.

Fate had been a cruel mistress these last few months. Ronnie had finally gotten the promotion she'd wanted at the Tampa Big Cat Rehabilitation and Rescue Habitat, then she got an insane call from her sister, Golden. Her life hadn't been the same since.

Golden's boyfriend at the time had imprisoned her, and was convinced that if he bit her, she would change.

What did that mean?

Golden was in tears as she relayed the details of her captivity to Ronnie and was convinced her ex would find her again. The police were no help. The guy came from money, or the mafia, or some crazy shit like that, and the authorities didn't want to interfere. They had no choice, Ronnie quit her job the next day, and they'd been on the run ever since.

Now, she and her sister were in Texas, in some town no one had ever heard of. She felt moderately safe, but her life was too complicated for her to be in a relationship with anyone. But this soft-spoken, utterly gorgeous guy called to something in her in a way she'd never felt before.

"Goldie," Ronnie said when her little sister stopped at the end of the bar.

"They're animals out there tonight. Touching, grabbing, no kind of manners." Golden threw the small round tray she used for multiple drinks under the bar. "What's up?"

"That guy in the back corner," Ronnie said with her back to the room.

Golden leaned to see around her sister.

"Oh my God, don't look," Ronnie squealed, pulling her sister back upright.

A smile as big as Texas flourished across Golden's face. "Ronela Anne-Marie Garrison." She looked around, then lowered her voice. "Are you smitten with someone? I never thought I'd see the day. Well, in order for me not to flirt with your man, tell me what he looks like, please."

"He's a tall guy in a long black leather coat, light-skinned, low-cut fade, beautiful pale green eyes…" Ronnie said a little dreamily.

"Girl, stop." Golden closed her eyes and waved her sister off. "Beautiful green eyes, really? I can't with you."

"It's not like that. He helped me when I dropped a bottle."

Golden's teasing voice eased. "You okay?"

"Yeah, yeah." Ronnie waved it off. "There was this sharp pain in my head. I thought I was about to have one of my migraines, then it went away."

"Oh, shit. That would be the worst. You know Dickwad over there is looking for a reason not to pay you." She tilted her head to smile at the aforementioned Dickwad - their boss. "Thank God for tips."

Ronnie grabbed a few different bottles of alcohol and poured the liquid into a shot glass, then dropped two servings of each alcohol into a silver shaker and gave it three good shakes. Poured the contents over ice and added a cherry. "Give him this."

"Shouldn't that be a lemon?" Golden pointed toward the small red fruit.

"He didn't look like a lemon kinda guy. Anyway, just give it to him," Ronnie said before helping a Paul Bunyan-sized man who just stepped to the bar.

Ronnie didn't know why she put the cherry in the drink. It just felt right, if that made any sense. Now she almost felt embarrassed for sending a complete stranger a drink. The fine nuances of how to flirt missed her in high school and college. No one was ever interested in the tall, lanky bookworm with no boobs and glasses. With a little time in the gym, lasik, and a great push-up bra, she turned out all right.

Her sister took the Long Island Iced Tea to him. Along the way, a group of loud obnoxious guys grabbed her, causing her to spill a little of the drink. Ronnie moved toward the end of the bar, about to leave.

"Hey," Dickwad yelled from behind her.

Ronnie rolled her eyes and turned back. "What?"

"Check the beer lines." He pulled the beer tap. Nothing came out.

Ronnie looked out towards her sister, who had gotten away from the pack of men.

"Now!"

Ronnie rolled her eyes, then hit the swinging door to the back room.

CHAPTER THREE

Oz watched as Ronnie disappeared behind the swinging door. He sipped his favorite drink. Even if Ronnie couldn't read his mind, she already knew something about him that most people didn't know. He hated the tartness of lemons and limes. She sent him his favorite drink with a cherry, instead of the normal lemon. It seemed like a small thing, but to him, it was huge.

The waitress' light fruity smell had been increasing since she brought him the drink. The shifter crowd had become overtly aware of her. A few noses lifted into the air to inhale as she walked past.

Why was the little waitress working in this condition? If she were raised with Ronnie and thought she was human, then she may not realize what was happening to her. Nor why the men were reacting to her this way.

"Let go!" The waitress tried, unsuccessfully, to snatch her arm away from an obnoxious lion shifter. The same one who had been grabbing at her all night.

Beer sloshed over her white t-shirt and the table roared with laughter.

"Take it easy, Kitten." He pulled her into his lap. "We just havin' a lil' fun."

The girl poured the rest of the pitcher of beer over his head, then jumped from his lap. "My name's not Kitten!"

Oz didn't move, he watched as the feisty girl's shoulders shook whether from a chill or rage back toward the bar. He was leaning more toward rage. He liked the little sister; even not knowing who or what those guys were she stood up to them. It told him something about what kind of women Ronnie and her sister were. Strong and fierce.

That little altercation cost the young girl something. Her scent flowed over the bar like an orange blossom tree in a gale wind. A few of the shifters lifted their heads and inhaled the sweet fragrance. The entire night her smell had been faint, but now every shifter in this building and maybe a three-mile radius knew she was ready for the change. Ready to mate.

Sex with a first time female shifter was said to be the most primal experience a shifter could have. Most males longed for the opportunity, but never got the chance. Now here this girl was flaunting her status. This wouldn't end well.

Ronnie came back up front just as her sister stormed up to the bar. He couldn't hear what they were saying, but Oz could read lips just fine.

"Hey, hey." Ronnie caressed the young waitress' cheek. "What happened?"

The girl looked out toward the lion shifter's table. "Those guys are creeps." She rubbed her arms, then touched the door. "Look, I need some air. I'll be right back."

Ronnie squeezed her sister's arm before the girl walked through the swinging door. Then she cut her glare toward the men, before getting back to work. No doubt calculating a painful death for each and every man. He smiled from behind his drink. This one had a mean streak, he could tell that without reading her mind.

The lion wasn't laughing anymore; he dried himself with every napkin at the table. Finally, he threw the wet wads on the floor and pushed away from the table. Causing the legs of the chair to make a screeching, nails on blackboard sound. He nodded his head toward the lion dressed in military fatigues at the door.

The guy had been a statue all night. No drinks, no women, no socializing at all. He had to be a bodyguard or a sentry. Had Oz not been watching the lions so closely, he would have missed the subtle head movement. The large man eased his leg down from the wall, unfolded his arms and slipped out of the front door.

Ronnie kept looking between her watch, the back door, and the thirsty patrons in a steady cycle. It had only been ten minutes, maybe less, but the increasing worry on her face made him tense. A scuffle broke out at the door, Oz watched the men tussle and fight over a woman who didn't seem interested in either one. When he'd looked back, she was gone. He looked away for one minute - one damned minute! Where did she go? Of course, no one but him noticed that she was missing.

Oz squeezed through the patrons to make his way to the bar. When he didn't see her, he closed his eyes and expanded his mental prowess to hear everyone's thoughts at the bar. She'd given everyone an extra drink on the house before sliding out the back door. He opened his eyes, holding back a hiss as he glowered at the defensive lineman sized African-American man at the end of the bar. The bear shifter wanted his woman. He had a detailed plan on how he would corner her and force her to her knees. Just as he moved to teach *Yogi* some manners, a psychic blast knocked him to his knees.

Help!

If he hadn't gripped the edge of the bar, he probably would've been laid out flat on his back. He looked around in a quick 360, but no one, male or female, seemed to be in distress. There was no doubt about it, whoever screamed out needed help. Right now.

Oz staggered out a side exit door. To others, he might seem drunk by the way he swayed and held the wall. It would take a minute for him to gather his equilibrium after being hit mentally with a blast that singed the edges of his brain and rocked him like an atomic bomb.

The snow had stopped, but a light fog had settled over the area. He looked both ways, but no one seemed to be in need of help. Rarely did an assault happen in front of witnesses. He heard a scuffle nearby as he neared the side of the building. He ran, his heavy boots splashed through a slushy, melted ice puddles. As he neared the other side of the building, the meaty sound of flesh hitting flesh rang out clearly along with a female voice crying out. The woman's sobs spurred him around the corner just in time to see Ronnie stagger back, holding her cheek.

Oz's fingers slid inside his duster, grabbing two throwing knives. With quick efficiency, he flicked them toward the man who'd dared to lay a hand on his woman. Then everything seemed to happen so fast. Another man back-handed Ronnie and he must have used his shifter strength or at least some of it, because her head snapped around so quickly. Oz was afraid the bastard had broken her neck. The back door of the old Suburban closed, and the vehicle sped away. He watched as Ronnie's head bounced on the concrete.

Oz slid to a stop, knees dropping in the filthy puddle as he lifted her. "Hey." The words were just above a whisper.

He jostled her a little when he lifted her up. A wisp of air caressed his face when he leaned over her; she was still breathing. He pulled his hand away from her head, and it was covered in blood.

"Sonofabitch." Those bastards would pay for this. "Baby-girl, I'm going to move you."

She needed some kind of medical attention, but he knew he was her only hope. He slipped his arms under her knees and behind her shoulders, carefully lifting her up. The toe of his black boots wedged into the small opening of the back door of the bar. A bloody size thirteen boot print was left behind after he kicked it wide open.

CHAPTER FOUR

The back stockroom was a mess. Oz knocked empty cardboard boxes and trash bags out of his way, then he spotted a long metal table covered with what he presumed was new inventory of wine and beer. He needed to move the cases, but he didn't want to put her down. Who knew what kind of diseases she would pick up in this room. Oz stomped the boxes flat, creating a barrier from the sticky nastiness on the floor.

Oz laid Ronnie down. Her silence was making him nervous. "Hey, Baby-girl, you with me?"

She groaned, and he took that as a good sign.

He pushed the cases of beer and wine on the floor. The crash of breaking glass brought one balding man peeping out, holding his unzipped pants from an office door.

"What the hell?" The out of shape man squinted looking around.

Oz had just laid Ronnie on the table.

Get a first aid kit, Oz ordered telepathically. When he looked at the bald man's appearance, he added, *Get rid of the girl.*

When the man looked confused, he sent a psychic blast, which was just short of him yelling, *"Move yo ass, motherfucker!"*

The man jumped in the air like a bunny, then yelled something behind him as he zipped up his pants. A young woman scuttled out of the room, pulling down her miniskirt and wiping the wetness from around her mouth. It didn't do a thing to fix her smeared lipstick.

Less than a minute later, the chubby bastard held out a blue and white canvas bag to Oz. It looked much like a kids' lunch bag. Oz unzipped it and found nearly nothing inside.

"Shit," Oz mumbled as he rummaged through the few items inside. He was positive this thing had never been restocked. He pulled out a roll of gauze, then found two alcohol wipes at the bottom and prayed they weren't dried out.

He looked up at the blank-faced man. *Did you guys never restock this thing?*

"No. Why would I? I ain't running no hospital."

Oz took a deep breath before he actually hurt this man. With a mental push, he sent the man back into the office.

The blood from Ronnie's head had stopped flowing. He wadded up some gauze and ran water over it, then wiped away the dried blood from her face, neck, and hands. The cool material seemed to help bring her back a little. Her eyes remained shut as she whimpered.

He ripped open the alcohol pad and touched the large bruise on her forehead. She squirmed, then hissed. "Babygirl, stay still."

Oz ran his finger over the circular imprint on her cheek. That lion shifter had backhanded her with an insignia ring on his hand. He pulled out his phone and snapped a quick picture. That guy didn't realize what kind of hell was going to rain

down on him. He hit her and possibly marked her. Oz didn't
know if the mark was permanent, but for her sake he hoped
not. He dabbed it with the alcohol swab, and she hissed again.

Her eyes flew open as she bared her teeth. "That stings."

Sorry, Oz said telepathically.

Ronnie grabbed her head as she cried out, "What the
hell?!" Her eyes clenched down. "That hurts so bad."

Oz rubbed her shoulder gently. He wanted to console her
and make the pain stop, but all he could do was wait for her
to stop moaning. She'd done this twice tonight, and now he
was beginning to suspect that he was causing her pain.

"Sorry."

"Not. Your. Fault," Ronnie said through clenched teeth.
"Migraines."

Oz wasn't so sure that was all of it. He hadn't been able to
read her mind at any point tonight.

With her eyes still closed, she whispered, "Water."

Shit, why hadn't he thought of that? His eyes scanned the
trashed room of broken glass and beer and wine pooling on
the concrete floor. In the back corner, he spotted a tall stack
of plastic bottled waters. The throwing knife was already out
by the time he reached the cases of water. He sliced the thick
plastic film and a few bottles fell out as he grabbed as many
as he could carry.

Deep creases marred Ronnie's brow, and her eyes were
still closed. Oz opened a bottle. "Here."

Ronnie cracked open one eye and wiggled her fingers.

"Raise up a little bit." Oz touched her arm.

She took a deep breath, then pushed herself up. He helped
her, and she didn't pull away, "Thanks."

Ronnie eyed him warily before taking a sip, then closed
her eyes as she took a deeper swallow.

Oz took the bottle when she finished. "You okay now?"

It took her a minute before she answered, then finally she said, "Yeah. I think I am." She lowered her legs, slid off the table, wobbled and nearly hit the floor.

He grabbed her before she went down and held her close. "Maybe you need a hospital."

She moved her head side to side, then winced. "No hospital." She leaned back on the metal table, seeming to catch her balance. "I'm okay."

Only then did he release his grip on her. It felt like the sun had been removed from his otherwise cold existence. Of course the entire thought was ridiculous, but it didn't stop him from wanting her.

"All right." He held up his hands up in surrender, but his heart hadn't given in at all. "But where are you--?"

"Wait." She held up her hand to stop him when he followed. "You've been nice to me all night, but why are you helping me?"

Oz opened his mouth, then shut it. He'd never enjoyed speaking aloud, but maybe it was her head injury that was making it difficult to communicate with her mind to mind. This was the most he'd spoken aloud in a very long time. His voice sounded weird to his ears every time he opened his mouth. This time was no different.

"I'm Oz. Oz Zhang."

He didn't know why he told her his entire name. He usually told people Oz or Wizard. He often got a strange look because he had an Asian last name, but he looked like a fair-skinned, black man. He had no desire to explain his heritage, but in his heart, deep down, he wanted to start this relationship off on the right foot. He wanted this woman to know everything about him.

She smiled. "Nice to meet you, Oz Zhang." She reached out her hand. "I'm Ronnie Garrison."

That strange thrill went through him again as he held her hand. The sun had returned. "Ronnie, a pleasure."

"It's actually Ronela, but no one calls me that. God, why did I say that? Don't mind me." She pulled her hand from his and tapped her temple. "I think I'm concussed." She pushed herself away from the table and ambled towards the back door.

Oz followed behind her. "Where are you going?" Every time she stumbled, his hands flew out.

"The alley. Did you see where they took her?" Ronnie leaned against the backdoor frame, taking deep breaths.

Who was she taking about? Oz stepped into the dimly lit alleyway. "Who?"

"My sister." Ronnie looked at the dark puddles of blood on the concrete. She nearly fell over when she kneeled to pick up something in the blood along the curb.

All he wanted to do was help her, but he was relegated to the sidelines. He couldn't push her or try to take over either. Slowly she would learn to trust him, but until then he would be there for her.

Oz reached out to help her up. Ronnie eyed him dubiously before taking his hand. "Thank you."

"What did you find?"

Ronnie flicked blood away as she wiped the item. A sparkle of yellow flickered in the light. A gold bracelet with small charms dangled from her fingers. Her eyes filled with tears as she held the jewelry to her heart and looked down the empty alley.

"It's Golden's." Her lips tightened as she wiped away tears with the back of one hand.

"The waitress from tonight?"

She nodded. "I'm supposed to protect her, you know. She's my baby sister."

Oz didn't have a blood sister, but the women in the club were his family. He would kill any mofo who dared lay a hand on any of them.

Ronnie continued as if he wasn't even there. "I tried to fight them off. They were just so damned strong. Shit! I lost my baby sister." Her fingers tightened around the chain. "I need to go after them." She moved around him.

"Wait." His heart wrenched at the pain in her eyes. "Your sister."

"Golden."

"Golden," his voice softened. "Did she have her phone on her?"

"Are you kidding? She takes it with her into the shower. Why?"

"It might help us find her."

"No. Why are you trying to help me? As a matter a fact, why have you been helping me all night?"

The head tilt and brow lift were so damned cute, he didn't answer. He could only stare. What was he going to say? Something about her called to him. That if she hurt, he felt it. If she needed protection, he would be her shield? She was a strong and independent woman. This wasn't going to be easy.

"Well."

"You don't look like you're in any condition to fight those guys again." He waved at her bloody state.

She looked down at herself and her bloody hands and quirked her lips like she agreed but didn't want to.

"Golden is in serious trouble. I don't think the police can help her."

"No, no police." Ronnie shook her head and waved off the mention of the cops.

That was interesting. Normally, women were all for calling the police. His brothers could help, but she didn't seem too keen on accepting anyone's help at the moment.

Ronnie patted her pocket and pulled out her phone. "Shit!"

She ran her finger over a dark, cracked screen. A smile blossomed on her face when it lit up despite the damage. After swiping and pressing a few things, she held the phone to her ear. Pacing, she couldn't keep still as she waited. "Straight to voicemail. What now?"

Oz pulled out his phone and tapped the screen. "What's Golden's number?" He typed as she gave him the digits.

"Router…"

"I am Oz. The great and terrible."

"You done?" It was always a pain to talk to Router. The girl was smart, like genius smart, but damn, she was a pain with her quotes.

"Wizard, what the hell? I didn't think you had this number. Hell, I didn't think you knew how to use the phone."

Router had a way of getting on his nerves like a little sister, and he found himself doing things he hadn't done since he was a kid. Like rolling his eyes. "I got everybody's number. Now, listen. I need for you to track the number I just texted you."

"Got it. What's this all about?"

Oz wasn't about to get into this situation with her. He could hear Router tapping on her keyboard furiously. "How long is this…?"

"Done." She'd answer before he'd finished his question.

He could hear the joy in her voice when she cut him off. Whatever, as long as he got Golden's location.

The tapping sped up. "Oh, shit."

"What?"

"Whose number is this?" Tap, tap, tap. "They're traveling on back roads going toward Corsicana. You need me to send back-up? That damned tiger's around here somewhere…"

It would be nice to have a fighter at his back, but the prospect would never get to him in time. "No, I just need…" His phone beeped.

"I just sent you the GPS coords. I take it this is about a woman since you won't answer my question. Whatevs. Open the app and follow the red dot."

He followed her instructions. "Got it."

"Alright. I sent the info to Kitty. No need to thank me. Bye." Click.

"Can your friend help?"

Oz concentrated on the moving red dot, then touched the screen, moving it along the faint white line along the map.

"Oz."

A soft hand touched his. It'd been a long time since someone touched him freely. Maybe it was just her, but it felt damned good. He looked into her chocolate brown eyes and was nearly lost... again.

He cleared his throat before he spoke and it still came out rougher than he'd intended. "Excuse me."

She tapped the phone. "Did your friend find her?"

"Yes. Well, she found the phone. It's still moving. I don't…"

She lifted her hand, cutting off his words. "We're going to find her right?"

Oz closed his eyes and inhaled her scent. Even through the blood he could still smell her. He nodded.

"Thank you." She pulled her fingers away.

Oz was about to open his eyes, when Ronnie's scent got stronger and surrounded him. If he'd opened his eyes, he might have lost the moment and broke the spell, so he waited.

Soft, full lips pressed against his cheek. His cat rose to the surface. They were united in wanting this human. She was theirs, there was no doubt in their minds. Finally, he opened his eyes when she stopped kissing him, but she hadn't pulled away. It gave him hope that she found him attractive.

Her head tilted very cat-like as she studied his face. "Do your eyes do that often?"

Oz and the cat stared even deeper into her eyes, before shaking his head. "Only with you apparently."

They stood like that for what seemed like forever, but in order to really have what he wanted they needed to find Golden. "Get your coat, let's go find your sister."

"I have a car."

"My bike is faster."

CHAPTER FIVE

I nside the small office next to the bathroom, Ronnie grabbed a few things from the locker she shared with Golden. She shouldn't even call it a locker. It was a file cabinet she'd placed a lock on. The owner and manager were shady as fuck. The men told them when they started that they could leave their items in the owner's office. More than one girl had been on her knees in that office, and she was pretty sure they had some bad habits and sticky fingers. And Ronnie was sure after a good blowjob, the owner would let the girls have anything they wanted out of that office.

Ronnie and Golden didn't have much since they left Florida a few months ago, but she had to protect what they did have. Plus, if the owner knew she had these pretty babies... She pulled two pearl handled 9mm from the very back of the cabinet. The fat bastard owner would have pawned them in a minute.

Ronnie had found them under the bed when she was about eight or nine. Between online videos, an overworked mom, and a deadbeat dad, she taught herself how to use them.

"Wait one goddamned minute! They should be back

here," Dickwad yelled. "I know they don't expect to get paid for only working half their shift."

Ronnie rolled her eyes. It wouldn't take much for him to decide not to pay them. Since he was paying them under the table, he didn't have to if he didn't want to. She slid the guns into the holster; it settled the cold metal low at her waistline. Her long leather coat camouflaged the weapons.

"Bitch, you coming back to work or what?" Dickwad yelled from the stockroom.

Ronnie cleared out the locker, throwing everything into Golden's backpack. It was obvious their time in this small town was over. She had to think of a new plan once she got Golden back. And she *would* get her baby sister back.

Golden had been through so much with her stalker ex-boyfriend. She hoped this had nothing to do with him, but deep in her gut she knew the truth. Santiago had his hand in this somehow. Who else would snatch a girl off the street like that?

Ronnie put the lock in her pocket and girded herself for a confrontation. She stepped out into a quiet stockroom; it was also a clean stockroom.

"What the…"

A woman wearing the same outfit she had on now, but blood free, followed Dickwad back into the bar area. Ronnie blinked; the girl - gone, and the room looked a mess as it did before.

"Hey. You okay?"

Ronnie looked between Oz and the still swinging door. "Yeah, yeah. I'm fine."

He leaned against the open back door. "You ready?"

"Yes? Did you just see that?" What did she just see? She must have a concussion because she was seeing things.

He hunched his shoulders. "What?"

Ronnie looked at the door to the bar again. Ultimately, she knew one thing, no one in this building cared about her or Golden. "Never mind. I'm ready."

When they reached his motorcycle, he held out a helmet to her.

Ronnie moved the helmet from side to side, looking it over like it was a UFO. "What about you?"

"I'll be all right."

She lifted an eyebrow.

He smiled. "Honestly, I'm tougher than I look."

It took a lot to hold back the laugh. Ronnie lifted both eyebrows as she said, "I'm sure you are, but it's not good if I'm wearing it and I hit you in the back of the head, then we're both dead. So, no." She tapped the helmet twice.

"I'm trying to protect you."

"Me? Didn't I just explain... look, you wanna protect me? Drive carefully."

He gave her a nod of acquiescence and her heart skipped a beat. She turned around quickly, not really knowing what to do with the helmet. "We can put this in my car. And..." She rummaged thought the backpack. "Here, it's cold." She handed him her skull cap and pulled Golden's knit hat over her own head.

After throwing his helmet into the old beat-up car she 'picked up' in Louisiana, she eased onto his bike. She'd never been on a Harley. A dirt bike when she was a kid, but that hardly counted. The leather seat was cool but molded to her butt like an old broken-in chair. She didn't touch him, instead she grabbed the metal under the seat behind her.

Oz looked around at her. "That's not going to work." He grabbed her hands and wrapped them around him.

"Oh, I forgot my gloves."

"Hold on to me. I'll keep you warm."

Ronnie rolled her eyes. Men! Keep her warm, sure.

Even through his coat, her hands ran over his trim, hard body. His body trembled under her touch. Men this gorgeous didn't react to her, but maybe her hands were cold. Her gloves were in the bag, but he was right, she didn't need them. Holding on to him was like kissing the sun. This man's body was a furnace. Holding him like this was a special kind of torture. The good kind.

He turned slightly and handed her his phone. "Watch the signal. Check it every thirty minutes or so. We should catch up to them soon."

She took the phone from him and looked at the small red dot. "Okay." Every thirty minutes? She wanted to stare at it until her sister was standing right in front of her. "Aren't you afraid I'm going to see texts from your other women?"

"What other women?" He kicked his foot down to start the motorcycle. The engine revved loudly. "Hold me tight. This baby can fly."

The bike took off. Her words were lost in the wind. "I thought you were going to go slow!" Her hands tightened around him.

If she died tonight, it would be in the arms of a gorgeous man.

THE BEASTLY MACHINE reverberated through Ronnie's body. So this was what a motorcycle felt like. She closed her eyes and reveled in the feel of power between her legs. Her thoughts drifted and wondered what it would be like with Oz. She wasn't a virgin by any stretch of the imagination, but she'd never met anyone like him before. He had a quiet way about him and a strength she admired.

It made her want to know more about him. How he liked to be touched; liked to be kissed; his favorite position; if he wanted to be on top; if he would let her be on top.

Lord, had it been that long since she'd gotten laid? That had to be it. That's why she was undressing and sexing this man without knowing a thing about him.

Ronnie loosened her grip a little and raised her head from his back. His scent was more intoxicating than any drug. Between that and his warmth, it also had to be playing a part in why, during all of this, she was thinking about him and not her sister. With that, she checked the phone.

For the last two hours, the signal seemed to be going in a circle, hitting every no name town in East Texas. Either they were trying to make sure no one was following them or they had no sense of direction. From what she remembered, there were only guys in the SUV. She could believe they wouldn't stop to ask for directions.

A phone vibrated in her pocket. She thought it was his and reached into her left pocket, and the screen was blank. The pulsation continued in her other pocket, where she'd placed her own phone when this search began. She quickly put his phone away, then snatched her own out.

The wind whipped all around her and she could barely hear, but she knew that number.

"Golden! Is that you? Hello." Ronnie patted Oz's stomach.

He pulled over without her having to explain why. But he must have heard her.

Without the noise of the bike and wind, Ronnie heard a slight tremor through a whispered familiar voice.

"Ronela."

CHAPTER SIX

"Golden!" Ronnie hopped off the bike, yelling into the phone, plugging her other ear with her finger. "Goldie, where are you? Are you okay?"

"I don't know where we are. Lots of trees. You have to help us."

"Bitch!" A man's voice growled. "What's that in your hand?"

"Give it back. You can't…" Golden screamed.

The slap of a hand against flesh echoed through the phone.

"Dude, you didn't fucking check her?"

Silence.

"Goldie!" Ronnie looked at the phone, then put it back to her ear. "Goldie?" But the phone was dead.

Ronnie's body quaked with wracking sobs. In those few seconds, her entire world had shifted. Some monster had her sister, and she had no way of saving her. Oz's crisp, minty scent calmed her. At some point, he took the phone from her hands. Now her arms were filled with this man. A man she didn't really know, but his very existence was the only thing keeping her sane.

Once she cried herself out, she wiped her cheeks dry. She never cried this much, but since meeting Oz, that's all she seemed to do. This man had seen her at her lowest and hadn't abandoned her on the side of the road. She couldn't help but wonder why he was sticking by her through this. He must have something better he could be doing. She would have to ask him later. If her life wasn't such a mess, she would like to hang around to get to know him. This man was loyal and genuine. That was something worth fighting for.

"Sorry about that."

Oz rubbed a hand up and down her arm. "Don't worry about it. What did she say?"

"Nothing really, before the guy slapped the phone out of her hand. Just that she was near a lot of trees. That's every place out here." She waved a hand around the miles of trees surrounding them.

Oz nodded, then held out his hand. "Can I have my phone?"

After she gave it to him, he touched the screen, tapped a few things, then looked around. "C'mon, we might just catch up to them." He caressed her cheek. "She's still alive and we'll find her."

Ronnie heard the words, but at this point she was losing hope and fast. Knowing her little sister was in this situation and she couldn't stop it or fix it - hurt her. She wasn't broken, but she was drowning in a sea of helplessness and that was pretty damned close.

A firm finger lifted her chin, and he didn't speak until she looked into his pale green eyes. She marveled at how much they reminded her of the big cat's eyes back at the wildlife sanctuary.

"Trust me. We'll find her," he said.

Something inside her cracked open as she looked into those depths. He had a resolve she didn't have right now. A fierceness that mirrored her own, although it was hidden right now. He seemed to know something she didn't know, but she believed him. They would find Golden. She just knew it.

Without thinking, her hands reached up and pulled the beautiful man standing before her to her eye level. They each seemed to instinctively know which way to lean as their lips met. He didn't know it, but she was known for bumping her forehead while leaning in for a kiss and knocking a guy out.

He'd opened for her and let her control the kiss. Ronnie slacked up, but Oz's arms wrapped around her and pulled her in tighter, reigniting the heat simmering between them.

Finally, Oz pulled back. The intensity in his eyes burned through her, and she felt like she could have melted on the spot. When was the last time she was kissed like that? Had she *ever* been kissed like that?

"I do trust you. Now, let's go save my sister."

LESS THAN THIRTY MINUTES LATER, Oz and Ronnie stood in a rest stop parking lot along the side of the highway. Oz held remnants of a broken cell in his hands. He turned the handful of pink pieces toward Ronnie. "Your sister's?"

She touched a few of the shiny, broken rhinestones, then picked up a large, gold colored, plastic 'G'. She held it over her heart and nodded.

It took her a full minute before she spoke. "What are we going to do now?" She looked around the rest stop. "I don't even know where we are!"

Oz looked around as well. He had a good idea about their

location but wasn't positive. He walked further along the walking path. The faint scents of more than just Golden still flittered through the air.

"Stay here. I'm just going to look around."

She mumbled something inaudible and turned away from him. Maybe that was for the best. The scent of so many girls engulfed the area. The more recent ones were like Golden, nearing the first change. Grabbing these girls at this point before their transition was dangerous. They would only snatch pre-shifter girls at this point for one sick reason. Selling them now was something equivalent to a turn of the century virginity auction.

As he walked further down a worn, muddy path, the fresh odor of at least four lions bombarded his senses. Old odors intermingled with the new from others marking their territory. This was bad. Hell, it was worse than bad, this was downright dangerous. Every one knew lions dealt in the skin trade. Sex slaves, prostitution, hits, and abductions was the least of their crimes.

The wind also carried something else, the sour smell of blood. Lots of it. His hand covered his nose automatically. The stench prickled his nose and made his eyes water.

Death. His leopard had been at attention since they found the phone. He sat ready to strike if needed.

They both knew what was beyond the copse of trees. With two fingers he lifted a torn yellow, tie-dyed t-shirt from a branch. He'd stepped off the path, through some evergreen bushes. The blood of a fresh kill was something he would never forget. His boots crunching down on broken branches seemed thunderous. The smell grew stronger and hung thick in the air.

A small muddy section was just ahead of him. He couldn't even call it a clearing. Just enough room to lay a body… or hide one. He moved a patch of large broken tree limbs to reveal the battered and broken body of a young girl. Blood matted her hair and her facial features were indistinguishable. Claw slashes marred the body across her exposed breasts down her torso. The material of her skirt was hiked up around her waist like a scarf.

A small light flickered behind him. "What are you doing?" Ronnie's gasp cut through the dead silence. "Is that? Is that my sister?"

He whipped around to see her wide-eyed stare. Her body trembled as she stood stock still. Her phone slipped from her hand, landing face up, illuminating the girl's feet.

"No, it's not her."

His arms were around her, pressing her face to his chest, trying to block her view of the body. He'd told her to stay back at the parking lot for just this reason. But his friend, Wraith, president of the East Texas Dark Leopards, told him on more than one occasion - women seldom do as they're told.

"How do you know?" She jostled in his arms in an effort to look around him, but he held her firm. "I need to see."

"No, you don't."

Oz knew in that moment he wanted to protect this woman. Shield her from all the cruelness in the world. It wouldn't always be possible, but in this thing… right now, he could. He turned her around by her shoulders and picked up the phone, dousing the light.

"Maybe, she's not…" Ronnie turned to look back again.

"She's gone. I'm sorry."

The tears had been streaming down Ronnie's face even though she wiped at them fiercely. When they reached the clearing, her knees seemed to give out from under her. With ease, he lifted her off her feet and sat her on the damp metal picnic table.

It broke his heart to see her like this. He wiped away the tears with his thumbs. It would take her a few minutes to process the horrible scene she just saw, and he let her have the time.

Console. His leopard raked him, displeased that he hadn't hugged her yet.

Give her a minute, Oz told him.

Why?

She needs this.

"Oz."

Ronnie's soft voice brought him back to the here and now. Their eyes met, and he grunted something unintelligible.

"I just don't understand. What kind of monster does that? She was just a baby."

Oz moved to stand between her legs, then pulled her into his arms. She held him tight, squeezed him, then pulled back to look up at him with a stern glare. The look sort of reminded him of the terminator, serious and all business with red-rimmed eyes, but no more tears.

"We can't let that happen to Golden. Promise me." She grabbed the lapels of his coat and pulled him, imploring him.

"Promise."

Her look of strong-as-steel determination galvanized something in him. He probably shouldn't have promised this one thing. It could break them apart before they even got started, if this ended badly.

"Call your friend. See if there's anything we can do to find them now!"

"Them?" How could she possibly know there was more than one female here?

"Goldie said, 'you have to help us.' That has to mean

those lowlives snatched more than just my sister. That girl," she pointed toward the trees, "may have been one of the last people to see my sister alive. Who knows what we'll find at the next rest stop?"

Ronnie jumped off the table. "We're getting my sister back and I'm going to kill every one of those sons of bitches." And with that she headed towards the motorcycle.

Oz smiled. Both he and his cat swelled with pride. This woman had had a rough night, but through the tears, fears, grief, and sadness it looked like she'd found her strength. Seeing that girl's broken body really did something to the both of them. He couldn't let those lions get away with this.

No matter what.

CHAPTER SEVEN

"The secret of getting ahead is getting started.' You know who said that?" Router spouted instead of a hello.

"Mark Twain."

"Strong, silent, and smart." Router feigned being cold. "Brrr, giving me the chills just thinking about it."

"Router," Oz said warningly.

"He used to be silent," Router mumbled under her breath, then continued, "Yeah, I've been watching, and I found some things. All those small towns they've been driving through, girls as young as thirteen have come up missing. One here and there. The police listed them as runaways. I'm not so sure."

"They were shifters around their first turn," Oz stated factually.

"Can't be a hundred percent, but yeah, it looks that way," Router said.

"Damn it," Oz said more to himself and it came out like a hiss.

"Exactly."

"Hotel. Ronnie's tired and I need to regroup."

"Sure. I'll send it to you, and I'll reroute that kitten to you."

"I'm going to send you a pic. I need to know who it belongs to."

"Gotcha. Send it over," Router said.

Oz didn't bother to say goodbye. He swiped the phone and sent the picture of the imprint on Ronnie's face. Within a minute, a beep let him know he'd received a text message. He opened it to find a map to a motel about forty-five minutes away.

"Ronnie," he called out.

She stopped pacing near the motorcycle. "Anything?"

"Well, Router's checking on a few things. We should hear something soon, but it's almost dawn."

"You must be tired." Ronnie grabbed his hands and squeezed them. "I appreciate everything you've done."

The depth of misery in her eyes decimated his heart. His cat nudged him.

Hold.

This time he agreed with his cat and pulled Ronnie into his arms. He took in her scent and both he and his cat found contentment. She was home.

With her head against his chest she said, "We need to call the police."

What? He didn't understand. When he offered to call the police before, she was categorically against it. Now, for this dead girl... Ronnie didn't flinch.

She looked up at him without tears, but a great deal of determination etched on her face. Then she pointed toward the trees. "For her."

"We will. Once we're outta here."

She spoke softly, more like to herself. "That could be Golden at the next rest-stop. Dead."

"Don't think like that," Oz responded quickly.

"How can I not?" She wiped away the flowing tears. "I'm sorry. Honestly, I'm not a weepy person. But that's all I've done around you. I just need to find her."

"I know. Com'on." Oz held out his hand, and she slid her fingers into his.

In this moment, he wished he was actually the wizard the club had dubbed him. There were very few vehicles out on the road. The misting had stopped, and the roads were only a little damp now. There weren't any signs of rain, snow, or even flurries in this part of Texas.

They arrived at the motel to find a long-legged man dressed in all leather, kicked back on his motorcycle. The young prospect looked like a real biker badass. Things were about to get really interesting.

"BOUT DAMNED TIME." The prospect peeled his long legs from his bike. "Router said you'd be here five minutes ago. Boy, she's gonna be pissed when I rub it in that she was wrong." He slapped hands with Oz, then put his hands on his hips as he looked Ronnie over. "And who is this?"

A small growl filled the air. Oz didn't like the way the young tiger looked at his woman. He slid in front of the man, blocking his view.

She doesn't know about us. Lock that shit down and be nice.

The young man inhaled with his eyes closed. *You sure about that? She smells a little like a tiger.*

"Is he okay?" Ronnie whispered from behind Oz.

Oz turned his head slightly, stating, "Yes, he's a little weird, but we keep him around, anyway." He turned back. "You done?"

The prospect tilted his head and winked.

"Ronnie this is…" Oz looked at the young tiger and decided on, "Kit. Kit, Ronnie. He's here to help us find your sister." She didn't need to know that they called him Kitty or why.

"Oh," Ronnie stepped around an unmoving Oz and extended her hand. "Hi. I appreciate you coming out."

Kit reached out, but another warning growl cut through the air, and he lifted both hands.

Ronnie looked between the two men as she lowered her arm. "Did you just freaking growl?"

Oz didn't answer, and Kit smiled.

"Any chance I can get to kick some li—bad guy's butt, I'm all in," Kit said.

"So, you're a fighter?" Ronnie asked.

"One of the best." Kit preened.

"Yeah, yeah. Let's not get him started. Look, let me go get us some rooms."

"Already covered." Kit held out a non-descript, dirty credit card sized plastic key. "You know Texans can't drive in this kind of weather. This place is booked solid."

Kit walked toward a set of rooms in front of their bikes. He swiped the card. The light on the door mechanism turned green, and he pushed the door open. He headed straight for the king sized bed and jumped on it like a little kid. The bed groaned under his weight, but it didn't collapse.

Oz and Ronnie entered behind him and sat at the two brown and beige striped chairs near a small round table.

"Wow, that wallpaper is something," Ronnie said, touching the wall.

"So, Ronnie. What do you do when you're not chasing down kidnappers?" Kitty said.

"Kit," Oz said with a bit of a growl.

"What?" Kitty looked between the Oz and Ronnie. "It's a valid question."

"It's okay." Ronnie reached out and tapped the table between her and Oz. "I worked at a wildlife sanctuary."

"They have those in Texas?" Kit sat up.

"I don't know; they might." Ronnie looked away.

Kitty met Oz's eyes. *She was hiding something.*

What, you can read her? Oz didn't know how he felt about that.

Well, you know. I can feel her emotions… her hesitation. Wait, you can't read her mind? Priceless. The smile on the young man's face was as wide as Texas.

It took a few times to understand that he was causing Ronnie's intense migraines when he tried to read her mind or talk telepathically to her. Oz reached out and slid her hand into his.

"Ronnie, whatever it is, you can tell us. We're here to help you. Trust. Remember?"

Ronnie winced, then said, "I know. It's hard. You guys gotta understand. It's just been us for a while now."

Oz squeezed her hand. "But you have me now and my family. That's why Kit's here. We will help you. Protect you." *Love you.* Those last words popped into his head unbidden.

The big tiger on the bed made a noise as he moved around. When Oz finally broke eye contact with her, he saw the prospect grinning. For the first time in forever, he wasn't able to control his feelings. Ronnie had no way of knowing, but his emotions were all over the place, and were pouring out of him like a waterfall.

"Yeah, Ronnie. We want to help," Kit said.

Ronnie looked between both of the men. "I don't know what I did to deserve you guys but thank you." She gave them both a brilliant smile and squeezed Oz's hand again before releasing it. "Trust. You got it. Me and my sister are from Florida. Before all of this happened, I was a Wildlife Rehabilitation Specialist."

"That sounds interesting but boring." Kitty scooted back on the bed and leaned against the headboard.

"What? No. I got to work with big cats every day. It was awesome."

Ronnie's enthusiasm was infectious. Oz found himself smiling right along with her as she talked about her job.

"Big cats?" Kitty lifted both brows toward Oz. "Really? Now, that does sound exciting. Doesn't it, Oz?"

Oz was not amused at the prospect, but his joy didn't diminish where Ronnie was concerned.

Ronnie turned to him with excited eyes. "You like big cats as well?"

"I feel at home around them, yes," he said to Ronnie, but inside he was just about ready to kill a tiger.

"Which were your favorite?" Kit asked.

"Wow, I worked with them all." Ronnie leaned back in her chair and looked thoughtful as she tapped her lips with her index finger. "I would have to say tigers were my favorite. They're so majestic and graceful."

"What!" Kitty practically roared. "Mine, too." His eyes gleamed with mirth. *Dude, I like her. I might even be in love.*

Just keep pushing, little kitten.

Oz's phone beeped, indicating he'd received a text. He opened his phone and scanned over all the info Router had just sent to him. He'd missed whatever else Ronnie had said, he only heard the enthusiasm wane in her voice.

"I don't know if I'll ever get to see a big cat again, let alone work with them."

"Why not?" Oz asked as he sat his phone on the table.

Ronnie looked at him and nodded like she was saying yes to something in her mind. She stood up and wrung her hands over and over. "You guys deserve to know everything." Ronnie began to pace from the front door to the bathroom door. "This isn't the first time my sister has been taken. Her ex-boyfriend, he took her. It took me a week to find her."

"Did he ever say why he took her?" Oz asked.

"You gotta understand, this boy was unstable. My sister said he kept going on about biting her and changing her. Who says shit like that? Bite her? Change her? Into what? That's what I always wondered." Ronnie sat down and put her head in her hands.

"But he never bit her?" Kitty chimed in very low.

"No. He kept telling my sister it wasn't the right time."

You hear this shit, right? Kitty looked at Oz.

Oz gave a slight nod. "Ronnie, how long ago was this?"

"I don't know. About three months, maybe four. Why?"

Oz didn't answer but asked another question. "Do you remember his name?"

"Sure. Santiago, Santiago Leonidas."

Oz and Kitty looked at each other. Ronnie looked at them both. "You know him." Not a question.

When neither said anything. Ronnie stood in front of Oz and pulled his face up to look hers. "You know him, don't you?"

Oz laid his hands over her cold ones. "Not personally."

"Tell me. What's the deal with him? Who is this guy?"

Ronnie stared him straight in the eyes and his cat felt like she was challenging him for dominance. Oz kissed the center of each palm and pulled her into his lap.

Kitty's phone rang. He looked at the screen, then said, "I gotta take this." He said telepathically, *It's Router. Come next door when you're done.* Then shut the door behind him.

"Tell me," he picked up his phone, "do you recognize this?"

Ronnie took the phone out of his hand and scrutinized the symbols and slashes with an old English styled 'L' in the middle of it. "Sure, I've seen it before. My sister used to doodle something like it on her notebooks all the time."

"Okay." Oz took the phone from her and sat it down. He made a point of showing her the ink and paper logo and not the picture of the ring imprint from her cheek.

"What does that mean? What does that have to do with my sister?"

"I just wanted to confirm we were searching in the right place. The thing is this, Golden's boyfriend comes from a terrible family. They deal in everything from drugs to prostitution."

"Shit. I told Goldie something was wrong with that boy."

Ronnie moved to get off his lap, but he held her in place. "I know this seems weird, but is your sister, by chance, adopted?"

The crease in her brow told him he was off base, but his nose didn't lie. She was human and Golden was definitely a shifter. Something was amiss in their family tree.

"What? No. Same Mom-Same Dad. Although I remember them fighting a lot right after Goldie was born, then dad disappeared."

"I'm sorry. I wasn't trying to bring up bad memories, but there's something about your sister you might need to know before we find her."

Ronnie tensed up as she stared at him. When she eased off his lap, he didn't stop her. She stood with her arms folded under her breasts. He recognized the defensive stance, but he remained seated.

"How could you possibly know anything about my sister that I don't already know?"

How do you explain that a person you've known your entire life is actually another species? He could see the suspicions and unrest building in her.

"Has Golden always been agile? Healed easily?"

Ronnie's brow eased as a smile inched out. "Yeah."

"Always seemed to be really hot, but never sick? Maybe even some special power?"

"Yes. She always seems to know what card you're going to pull or what numbers dice will land on. My mom said she got it from our dad, but I was never good at guessing games and I always got sick. What's that got to do with anything?"

Oz stood and pulled her arms away from her body, loosening her fingers, then intertwining them with his. "When we find your sister, she might be changed."

"How?"

"Mentally and physically, she'll be changed. She won't be the little sister you knew before."

"Oh, oh…" Ronnie pulled out of his hands and covered her face. "You mean, they could…" she didn't even finish the sentence.

He was really botching this. "No, no. Of course, we'll find her before anything like that can happen."

"I understand and I love her. No matter what they do to her, as long as I get her back. I don't care what she looks like. She's my sister."

"Good." He wasn't about to try to explain actual physical changes. He just hoped she was true to her word. "Why don't you take a bath? I want to see if Kit found out anything from Router."

He kissed her on both cheeks. Those baby kisses must not have been enough for either of them. They both went in for another kiss and bumped heads. Oz winced and rubbed the point of infraction.

"Owww." Ronnie held her forehead. "Okay, that means I'm tired. You'll tell me, right? If you find out anything?"

"Of course." He watched her as she walked toward the bathroom. When the door shut, and the water started, he walked out to find that loud-mouthed tiger.

CHAPTER EIGHT

The room next door looked exactly like as the one he was sharing with Ronnie. This motel must have gotten a deal on the cardinal and blue jay with branches motif wall paper.

Oz paced back and forth over the threadbare burgundy carpet.

"Dude, you need to chill." Kit lounged against the headboard of the king-sized bed. "She'll call back soon."

"Isn't she normally faster than this?"

The prospect ignored his question and asked, "So… Ronnie?"

Oz stopped in his tracks and glared at the young man. "Don't."

The young tiger seemed oblivious to Oz's growing hostility, either that or he didn't care. He continued to speak with his eyes closed. "Hey, man, I know she's human, but she's hot."

A growl filled the small room.

Kit's eyes popped open, and his hands went up. "Why so protective? I'm just making an observation."

Oz's cat came to the surface and his voice dropped an octave as they both said, "Don't observe."

Kit sat up and stared at Oz, then inhaled. A huge smile spread across his face. "Could it be? The solitary, 'I don't need nobody' snow leopard has found his mate? A human no less."

Oz broke eye contact and all his animosity left him in a big whoosh. He fell into the nearby chair. "Let's not talk about it."

"Come on. This is great news. So, you tell her yet?"

Oz frowned and looked away.

"Okay, I can tell by the grief pouring off of you, you haven't. But you have to tell her about you. Hell, about all of us."

"I tried."

"Try harder. You need to. You can't keep that kind of secret from your mate. You are planning on mating her, right?" Then Kit looked away and licked his lips. "If not, I'd like for her to get to know my big tiger."

That sonofabitch just licked his chops. He's fucking thinking about my woman. An irrational flood of jealousy rolled over Oz. He wasn't sure if it was him or his cat.

Our woman. Kill. Now.

Before Oz knew what had happened, his cat had taken over.

A very animalistic growl came from Oz as he leaped across the room and wrapped his hands around the prospect's throat when his phone rang.

Kit smiled, then choked out, "You might want to get that."

Oz jumped off the annoying cat and answered his phone. "What?!"

"Hello, Sunshine. I guess you must be talking to that lovely kitten of ours if you're in this good of a mood."

"Router," Oz said her name warningly.

"Fine. King, the leader of the Demon Lion Pride has a place in Houston, but after an *anonymous* tip, the police checked it out. Nothing. The place was clean. Look, I can't tell you exactly where the lions are holed up, but you are close to a state park. I think if anything, they're somewhere in there. I sent you coords to the best possible part of the area. You should look there first."

"Got it." Oz hung up and looked at Kit. "It was Router," he mumbled.

Kit gave him a lazy smile. "I heard."

"Look. About what just happened…"

Kit held up his hands. "All forgotten. But maybe you should mate her before she meets someone who actually is interested in getting to know her."

Oz knew he was telling the truth. He would tell her soon. When the time was right. Maybe after all of this was over and she had her sister back. "I'll meet you near the tree line out front. It'll be faster if we shift."

WHEN RONNIE FINISHED HER BATH, she couldn't bring herself to put her filthy clothes back on. She wrapped herself in the top sheet and tied it toga style. She pulled the clean, empty bag out of the small trash can and threw her dirty clothes into it.

Bold as brass, in her stylish pale blue sheet and floral comforter cloak, she walked to the office. The older woman with a blue coiffure behind the desk reached for the neckline with wide eyes.

"Hello," Ronnie said with a smile. "Could you help me?"

"Get in here, girl. You gon' catch your death from cold." The lightly blue-haired lady waved her in.

"I messed up my clothes pretty bad and I was wondering if I could use your washing machine?"

"Oh, yes, dear." The woman pulled her half moon eyeglasses down and they dangled around her neck by a metal chain. She held her hands out. "I can do it for you."

"Oh, no, ma'am. I can do it if you just point me…"

"I can't have you catch your death running around out here in a sheet. Please."

It bothered her to let this woman do her laundry. She nibbled her bottom lip as she considered her options.

"It's not a bother, really. Besides, I've seen this episode of Midsomer Murders." The woman held out her hand.

Ronnie knew she didn't want to put the clothes on, and Oz was still talking to Kit. She handed the plastic bag over. "Thank you so much. I'm Ronnie by the way."

"Berniece. A pleasure," she said as she took the bag of clothes.

Ronnie told her the room number and Berniece said she'd send them back once everything was dry. She hurried back to the room and sat on the bed. Her plan was to wait until Oz came back to let her know what their next move was going to be. She wasn't sleepy at all, even though she hadn't been to sleep since yesterday, before her shift twenty-four hours ago.

The pull of sleep was powerful. She'd fought it every time her eyelids closed; she'd forced them back open. But finally, she rested her eyes. A few minutes wouldn't hurt. Besides, Oz would wake her when he came back in the room.

Her dreams were vivid and clear. They had found her sister. Golden's hair was a frizzy, afro mess, but she looked good. They hugged, kissed, and cried. That scene sat on repeat for a few times. Then things changed. Golden wasn't around, but he was.

Oz.

Her tall, quiet knight in black leather, riding a two-wheeled silver steed. She watched his full kissable lips; they weren't moving but she could hear his baritone voice. The words were unimportant; it was what he was doing to her that was important. Her body felt like the heater had kicked on and her clothes were holding her hostage. Sweat beaded down between her breasts and she couldn't pull her clothes off fast enough.

Shirt and jeans. Gone.

Bra. Across the room somewhere.

Panties. Melted away.

She stood before Oz in all her naked glory. He didn't say a word, just licked his lips like a cat eyeing a big bowl of cream. She wanted to be that. She wanted his lips and tongue on her. It was his eyes; they reminded her of one of the big leopards at the wildlife sanctuary every time he stared at her for long periods of time. She pretended not to notice, but he stirred something in her soul every time he looked at her.

"Oz." His name came out a husky purr. "Touch me."

Never-mind that her hands had already begun to caress her extended nipples, displaying them out like an offering. He didn't touch her though. No, he walked around her, then blew a cool breeze against her hot skin.

From behind, he leaned in and nibbled her ear, then whispered, "You're so beautiful like this."

He plied light kisses down her neck, then bit at the junction between her neck and collar, just hard enough to make her squeal. Her other hand went lower. She had to assuage the need building between her legs.

His mouth and tongue were making her mindless. He

moved in front of her and kissed as he went lower on her body. When he took her hardened nipple into his mouth and she cried out.

"Oz!" Ronnie woke up screaming his name. She looked around the room, but she was alone.

Aroused nipples, sweaty body, and the sheet was bunched up around her waist. It was more than just a dream, this man had her worked up in ways she had never been before. She was still horny. Still wanted him to stop this need in her. No man had ever made her want him this badly without laying a finger on her.

Across the room on the small table was a paper bag and a drink. That wasn't there before. Her face fell into her hands. He'd been in the room at some point. How much did he see? There was nothing she could do about it now. If he didn't talk about it, she was certainly not going to bring it up.

The sheet was a rumpled mess. She shook it out and tied it back into a makeshift toga. Instead of turning on the light, she grabbed a couple of fries from the bag and opened the curtain. A flash of orange and black darted into the tree-line. Ronnie blinked, but didn't move a muscle. Not that the creature could see or smell her. Hell, she wasn't even sure about what she'd just seen. Just as she'd wiped the sleep from her eyes, the bushes moved along the trees. It wasn't orange this time, but a snowy white cat with pale black spots. No, rosettes.

"There's no way." Her stomach growled. "See, I'm hungry so, obviously, I'm hallucinating." Maybe it was all the stress making her lose her mind. A leopard and a bengal tiger running loose in the backwoods of Texas?

Not possible.

A part of her wanted to run after them. And do what? Get

mauled? Nope, she would stay put. Then another voice said in the back of her mind, "What if they need help?"

The first thing she did was call Berniece to see if there had been any reports of wild animals in the area.

"Ferals. Yes, we see those every once in a while. Oh," she chuckled to herself. "A couple of years ago there was a report of lions on the loose. Imagine that, lions in Texas. The police quickly realized it was a hoax. Kids making prank calls and all, but that's it."

Ronnie wasn't crazy, well, at least not completely, but she knew what she saw. She snatched up the chair and table and placed them by the window. With her feet kicked up, food in her hand, and a clear line of sight to where she last saw the cats, she waited.

She had to wait for Oz. Wait for her clothes to get dry. Wait for the cats to come back.

Big cats in the backwoods of Texas. Who would have guessed?

CHAPTER NINE

I t didn't take long to pickup the lion's scent. The tiger chuffed a few times, clearing his nasal passages, Oz suspected. He had to do the same. Lions straight up stank. The odors from where they marked practically every tree, branch and leaf pretty much led them straight to their lair. Router was right, not that he would tell her so, but the section she marked on the map was close to where they stood now.

A collection of faded rail cars were lined up on one end of the property and a stone walled, two story craftsman style home faced a large gladiator style arena.

Thoughts. Oz's mind was flooded with images of blood, murder, hunger, rape and escape. He concentrated more on the female thoughts.

Are they here? The tiger looked between him and the compound.

Oz shook his head, but kept listening. One thought stood out in particular. She prayed for her sister to find her, a lot of crying, praying, and then one name. Ronnie.

Sister.

I heard it, Oz said to his cat. *Golden? Can you hear me?*

A minute or two went by before the girl answered. *Yes?* The word came out in a low, almost imperceptible noise.

My name is Oz. You remember me from last night?

How are you doing this? Are you one of them? Golden said warily.

No - No. I'm with your sister. We've been looking for you, Oz whispered.

Is Ronnie okay?

Yes, now, tell me. Do you know where you are?

It's not just me. There are so many girls here. I don't know where we are, it's a metal box, I know that much. No lights or anything. They put bags over our heads. Are you really going to save us?

Yes. There was no hesitation. They would get her back.

Look. Golden's voice sounded closer to a whisper. *Something is happening to us. I'm scared. We all are.*

Just hang on.

The tiger loped back to stand next to him. *You find her?*

Oz lifted his head toward the three faded rail cars. *I think they are over there.*

Golden cut into his thoughts. *Please, hurry. They did something to me. I feel something moving around inside of me. It wants out.*

Shit! He thought to himself. Her time was near. *Can you hold on a little longer? It's the middle of the day. We'll come for you once it's dark.*

I think I can, but some of the others are panting and crying. They might die soon.

Oz knew they weren't dying, but he couldn't explain what was happening to them now. That might freak them out more than they already were. But if so many were this close to the change, the lions would have to move the product soon. They had to go in hard and fast.

Just hold on. We're coming for you.

The snow leopard backed away. *We're gonna need the bus,* he said to Kitty.

It's that many?

Sounds like it.

They ran back to the motel at full speed. Now that he knew it was more than one girl they had to rescue; this changed his plans a little bit. Oz and Kitty changed back before walking back to their rooms.

AN UNEXPECTED SIGHT came from the tree-line. Ronnie had hoped to see the big cats again. Her feet fell off the old floor AC unit, then she snatched the curtain wider to get a closer look.

Oz pulled his shirt down over his head and Kit didn't even have a shirt on as he pulled up his jeans, leaving the top button undone.

Couldn't they have been more discreet?

This entire time she thought Oz felt something towards her. A real connection.

Lies! All lies.

This was her fault. She had made up this attraction in her head, but it was just the stress of this whole situation. Ronnie swung open the door as the men stepped in front of the motel rooms.

"Boys." Ronnie was very proud of the fact that her voice didn't crack.

As she slammed the door behind her, she heard Kit say, "You got some explaining to do."

In her haste and maybe a little bit of flare for the dramatic, Ronnie forgot to lock the door. Oz hit the door with such force she thought it was going to come off the hinges.

"Ronnie, let me…"

"Just don't." She held up her hand to stop the cliché from falling from his lips.

He stopped in his tracks.

Ronnie walked into the bathroom, slammed the door, then two seconds later walked back out. "Why didn't you just tell me? That would have made this so much easier." At this point, Ronnie had a litany of things she wanted to say.

"Tell you what?"

"I mean I thought we had this connection, you know. Something special." She paced, not looking at him.

He stepped into her path. When she looked up he said, "Tell you what?"

"That you like boys!" Why was he acting obtuse?

His eyes went wide, like she had slapped him.

"Not that anything's wrong with that. I just don't like to share."

"Hell, I don't either and I don't like men."

"Wait. What?"

"You heard me."

She pointed toward the window. "Really? Because it looked like you were getting dressed after having a little slap and tickle with Kit."

"That's not what happened."

She folded her arms and tapped her foot. "Okay, fine. Tell me. And this better be good."

He seemed to mumble something along the lines of, "I didn't want to do it this way."

Ronnie had worked up a good mad. She knew there was nothing he could possibly do or say that would make her believe him. Her eyes seemed to go in every direction except toward him.

"Ronnie," Oz whispered. "Look at me."

She exhaled loudly before lifted her eyes to a man who she thought could be the one. It was stupid to think someone as gorgeous as him would really like her.

"Okay, what?"

CHAPTER TEN

How did everything get so fucked up? Oz had intended on coming back, maybe finishing what she was doing when he'd walked in on her earlier. Kissing her, touching her, loving her. At this moment, that seemed like such a far off possibility.

Ronnie's eyes were filled with despair and betrayal. He had only one choice. He needed to show her.

"I don't like Kit. I like you. I want you."

"Then why?" Ronnie's voice crack on the second word.

"Because it's difficult as hell to transform while still wearing clothes."

She shook her head, all confused. "What are you talking about?"

"This." Oz pulled his t-shirt over his head, then unzipped his leather pants.

"Wait. What are you doing?" Ronnie moved in close to him, like she was about to stop him.

"Stand back." His voice came out more of a growl than words. Changing into his leopard wasn't usually painful but doing it again this quickly was going hurt… bad.

After a few deep breaths, he dropped to all fours.

"What are you doing?"

His back bowed, and all of his bones and joints popped as they elongated. White hot magic burned over his skin in ripples as the fur emerged from his back just before his cat burst forth. A clear liquid splattered all over the carpet. The large white cat gave a shake, but his fur was completely dry.

Ronnie's eyes were huge as she fell backward, hitting the wall.

Oz was aware, but right now his cat was mostly in control. What he and his cat couldn't decide was, if she was afraid of them or not. Shock, yes. The wide eyes and lack of speech told them that much but nothing else. Only one way to find out. They took a step forward.

She whipped her hand out, halting him. "Wait. Stop." Her breathing had kicked up exponentially.

The big cat stopped, then laid his head down on his big paws.

"You're a snow leopard." It wasn't a question, more a statement of fact. "A fucking snow leopard."

He purred, and she smiled.

"Okay. I have to admit, not what I expected," she said more to herself. "And you can understand me?"

The leopard lifted his head a little, then nodded.

Ronnie rolled to her knees and stared into his eyes. "You. It's your eyes I've been seeing. The cat's."

She reached her hand out and the big cat scooted forward to touch it with his nose. A giggled bubbled up out of her.

Deep inside, Oz sighed. The connection between her and the cat was just as strong as his and hers. The cat licked her fingers.

"Oh, you like me," she said.

When they touched, it was like a circuit was finally

completed. He felt whole. She scratched behind his ear, and the cat purred. Oz's leopard had only ever been affectionate with his mother. Now, the cat laid on his back and Ronnie was rubbing his tummy.

"I had no idea. Wait, is Kit a snow leopard, too?"

Oz let out a growl and hissed.

"I'll take that as a no."

The leopard flipped over and stepped out of reach. Oz would like a belly rub his damned self. Changing back didn't take as long, and wasn't nearly as painful.

Ronnie watched with her mouth agape. Oz walked his very naked self to the corner where he'd discarded his shirt and pants. He cracked his neck from side to side. "Well, you believe me now?"

"I… um… wow."

Oz lowered himself to her level. Well, that was better than her running from the room screaming. "You okay?"

Ronnie nodded. "Can you talk in that form?"

He was amazed that was her first question. Although he'd never outed himself to a human before. He thought it would be something like, 'were you born like that or were you bitten?'

"Hmmm. I can. It's more mental." Oz stood up and reached out for her.

She took his hand without hesitation.

"Like in the movies. What's it called…" she snapped her fingers. "Telepathy."

They both sat on the bed facing each other.

"Yes, but it doesn't work on you."

Ronnie frowned, then asked, "You sure? How do you know?"

"I'm pretty positive."

"You've already tried. When?" Ronnie hit his leg playfully.

"When I first…" *realized you were my mate.* "Met you."

"And what happened?"

"Nothing. I can't read you."

"Try again. A lot happened that night. I'm mostly calm now. Try again." Ronnie gave him that smile that would guarantee her just about anything.

"I don't think…"

"Please." She clasped her hands like she was praying.

"Okay. Fine."

Oz had seen the results of his powers on her, and this would not end well. He didn't push too hard. *Ronnie, can you…*

"Oh, my God!" She grabbed her head and fell sideways on the bed.

"Dammit, girl." He jumped off the bed and ran into the bathroom. He ran cold water over a hand towel. "I told you it wouldn't work." He handed it to her when he came back into the room.

Ronnie took it and placed it on her forehead. She blew out a long breath. "It wasn't you. I've gotten migraines my entire life. Check my coat. I should have some aspirin in there."

Oz looked through one pocket and then the other. He lifted the coat, and it seemed heavier on one side. He reached into the interior pocket, and his fingers grazed the cool metal of two guns. He pulled one up just to confirm. The pearl handle gleamed in the soft room light. He slid it back and took the bottle of pills and a bottled water from the small table to Ronnie.

"You sure that I didn't cause this?" Oz frowned at her.

Ronnie took the two pills from his hand and then swallowed two big gulps of water. "I'm sure." She grabbed her head "Ow, ow."

"Did your migraines start when Golden was little? Maybe she was trying to tell you something?"

"Why would you say something like that? That's not..." She'd opened her mouth to deny it all, but he could see she really thought about it for a moment.

"Yeah, Golden would get mad, stamp her foot, then Bam! Headache. Wait, are you saying my sister is one of you?"

Oz nodded.

Ronnie shook her head. "That's not possible." She took three deep swallows of the bottled water and finished it.

"It is."

"So, you're telling me, my sister and I are leopards?"

"Um, I'm not quite sure what your sister is." He could tell she was a shifter, but that was it.

"When will I change? What am I?" There was a hint of excitement in her voice.

"You are very much a human."

She frowned. "That makes no sense. We have the same parents."

"I don't think you do." He hated to tell her this on top of everything else. But there was no other way to say it.

This was really bothering her; he could see it on her face. "Don't worry about that right now. Let's just concentrate on getting Golden back." She frowned, but after a minute she expelled a resigning sigh. "I saw on your note you had some leads. Do you know where she is?"

"Yeah, we found her."

"Oh, my God!" She yelped, then winced. "So when are we leaving?"

"Once it's dark. But Kit and I will go back to get Golden and the others."

All the joy Ronnie had a moment ago seemed to drain away as her arms slid from around his neck. "What about me?"

"I don't want you to get hurt. Plus, you're having migraines. Stay here." *Stay safe.*

"If it's not till later, I'll be fine." Ronnie sat up on the bed. "You are not leaving me out of this. I can't believe you. She's my sister."

"I know, but the men who have her are dangerous."

"What? Are they like you? Were-leopards?"

"I am a leopard shifter and no. They are fucking lions and they are murderers."

"I got something for them."

"I saw. Do you even know how to use those?" He knew that was a dick move, but he needed her to be safe.

"Yes. Have you thought about how you are going to get Golden plus the others away from where they are being held? No offense, but you can't lead them out in cat form or worse naked. These are scared kidnapped girls."

"My club should be on the way with the bus. It's an armored SUV. It will be big enough for all of them."

"Will they get here in time?"

"Let me check." He didn't pick up a phone but stared at the wall. *Hey, Kitty.*

Yeah, I'm coming.

"Are you doing the mental talk thing?" Ronnie asked from behind him.

Oz smiled. "Yep."

Kit opened the door without knocking. "Hey, kids, what's shaking?" He closed the door, but instead of walking in any further, he looked between them. Then stared longer at Oz. *Did you tell her?*

Oz answered aloud. "Yes, she knows everything. Now,

what did Router say?"

"They are sending the bus, but it might not get here in time." Kit sat in the available chair at the door. "They had to use it on another job."

"See, you need me." Ronnie preened.

"Wait. What happened?" Kit looked confused.

"She wants to come with us," Oz grumbled out.

"Awesome," Kit said with a smile.

Suddenly, a growl filled the room.

"Not awesome?" Kit looked at Oz. "She might come in handy. It's not like we can get the girls out while we're fighting."

Oz knew that, but he didn't want to put her in danger. She was only human. "I won't be able to protect you," he stated, looking at her.

"I'm not asking you to." Ronnie went to her jacket and pulled out two 9mm guns and held them upward. "I can take care of myself."

Kit jumped up to look at the weapons she held. "May I?"

Ronnie handed one of the guns to him.

Kit touched the barrel, admired the handle, then pressed the release button to check the magazine. "This is awesome."

"We don't have a vehicle."

"I can handle that," Ronnie answered with a smile. "I've had to *borrow* a few vehicles the last couple of months."

Her smile was a little too saccharine sweet. He was fairly certain she was going to hot-wire a vehicle from the parking lot.

Kit, give us a minute.

You know she's right. We'll protect her though. Those lions aren't shit. We can handle them. Kitty handed her the gun back. "I'll be back about thirty minutes before sunset." He winked at Ronnie. "I like your guns."

"After this is over I have a ton of questions for you," Ronnie said with a huge smile.

Oz thought the smile Kitty gave Ronnie looked more wolfish, and he growled after the prospect shut the door. "I don't know if I like that smile you have after talking to that tiger."

"What? I'm just curious." Ronnie smirked at his obvious agitation. "But that snow leopard is pretty gorgeous too."

"Gorgeous, huh?" He knew she was just placating him, but it felt damned good.

Oz took her hand and walked her to the bed. "I can't lie; I don't want anything to happen to you."

"But..."

"Let me finish." He put a finger over her lips to stave off any rebuffs. "You are human. I get that you can protect yourself, but the girls we are rescuing are close to the change. They could change while you are driving and injure you, or worse, you would have to shoot one of them. I don't want you to have to live with something like that on your conscience."

That seemed to give her pause as she considered what he'd just said. "I hear you. I do, but if it was me out there. Golden would do no less. If I had no one - I would hope someone would come save me. I couldn't live with myself if I sat here and did nothing."

When he opened his mouth to interrupt, she covered his lips with one finger, mimicking him. "I appreciate everything you've done for me. But this is something I have to do. I would prefer we do it together, but either way... I'm going."

And just like that, this strong woman in front of him had his entire heart. "Okay. Together, then. Now, we have a little time to kill, what do you wanna do?"

CHAPTER ELEVEN

"How much time?" Ronnie questioned as she slid her arms around Oz's neck.

The last twelve hours had been surreal. Who knew that shifters existed in this world? And now she stood in front of one of the sexiest men she'd ever met. The one thing that Ronnie had learned in the last few months, being on the run with Golden, was that tomorrow wasn't promised. She pulled Oz to her; the kiss was long, wet and deep.

She let out a little "Eep" sound when he snatched her up. Her legs wrapped around his waist and his large hands cradled her naked butt under the toga as he carried her to the bed. No-one had picked her up since she was a little girl. She'd gained the freshman fifteen in college and another twenty-five along the way. She wouldn't dare let anyone even try to pick her up for fear of them hurting their back. He lifted her like she was as light as a feather and laid her down just as gently.

It had been a really long time since Ronnie had found herself under a man. Oz must have sensed her hesitation. His hands stopped moving and he leaned off to the side on one arm as his eyes bore into hers. "We don't have to do this. Just say the word and we can watch TV."

Did she really want that? Hell, no!

She wanted this man, even if it was only for this one time. Instead of answering immediately, she took his free hand and grazed his finger over her breasts on the way to her waiting mouth. Her nipples perked up under the material at her decision, and so did he.

His body shuddered next to her, and his eyes dilated and the green darkened into that cat-like stare she now associated with his leopard. She felt like prey, but she didn't dare look away.

"Say the words, Baby-girl. I really need to hear you say them." The words were just short of a growl.

"I." She bit the tip of his index finger, still caught in his gaze.

"Want." Nibble.

"You." She sucked his entire finger into her mouth.

That was enough for him. In a blink, her makeshift toga flew over her head, leaving her completely naked below him. He looked her over from head to toe, then his mouth was on her. His tongue invaded as she surrendered. Giving him everything he wanted as he gave her everything she needed and more.

Moaning at the pleasure, she pulled at the hem of his t-shirt. She wanted him with an urgency she'd never felt before. He laid his hands over hers, making her release him, then lifted up, flexing his abs as he took the shirt off.

Ronnie raised up to her elbows to watch him. "Those too," she said in an even raspier sound than her normal voice.

Oz shook his head. "Not yet. Now lay back."

She complied, falling back like a kid into a swimming pool and he followed, but this time his lips made a trail down her neck, then to the one place that made her nearly buck him off her.

Behind her ear.

He pressed his hardening erection into her core as he grabbed both wrists, forcing her back onto the bed.

"A little sensitive, I see. I'll have to remember that."

"No," she gasped out. "No need."

The wicked smile that flashed across his face told her that wasn't going to happen. He gave her a quick nip behind the ear, and her body melted.

Oz stopped kissing her for a moment only to lower himself, placing his mouth over her breasts. It was like her nipples summoned him. He lightly ran the tips of his fingers over one nipple, then nipped and sucked on the other.

All of her nerve endings seemed to fire at once. If he continued at this pace, she was going to pass out. He gave each breast equal attention, then pressed his soft lips in tender kisses further down her stomach.

"No, you don't have to…" Ronnie jumped up.

She'd never had a good experience with oral sex, and she didn't want to be disappointed now. Given how exquisite everything had gone so far, she didn't want it to end.

"Woman, lay down. I got this." Oz pressed two fingers between her breasts and pushed her back down.

Before she could say another word, his mouth found her core. The first brush of his tongue against her sensitive bud had her crying out.

"Oh, God."

Over and over his tongue lashed the bundle of nerves at the apex of her sex, causing her to forget everything she thought she knew about the act of lovemaking. This was not what her previous partners had done. Oz was skilled and talented as he lapped at her wetness like a cat at a bowl of cream.

He lifted above her, holding one thigh as the other hand worked her where his mouth had just been. The pressure was building, and she wasn't sure how much longer she would last. He hadn't even entered her yet. What would she do then? The passion was almost more than she could bear.

"Oz, I can't…"

"You can't what?"

His fingers slowed, but didn't stop the rhythm.

Her breathing eased, but her mind fogged. What was it she couldn't do?

"Ronnie?" Oz whispered in her ear. "What can't you do?" He purred, and it vibrated throughout her entire body.

She couldn't remember why she was protesting so much. Her body responded to his every touch. "Nothing. I'm good."

"I can finish now?" His fingers never stopped rubbing her core.

"Yes," she panted out.

She grew wetter with every stroke. Her orgasm was close, so very close and just like that he removed his fingers. Ronnie groaned out her displeasure, but that lasted only a moment.

Oz slid his finger back inside her moving in and out of her repeatedly, then placed his mouth over the bud at the top of her sex and sucked.

Ronnie nearly jumped off the bed. "Oz. Oh, my God. That feels so good."

He used his tongue deftly as he licked and swirled through her folds. The pressure built and built until finally her orgasm rippled through her body and she covered her mouth to keep from letting the entire motel know what had just happened.

Oz crawled up the bed and cradled her in his arms. She wanted to tell him that was mind-blowing, fantastic, and earth-shattering. Instead, she yawned and curled deeper into his natural body heat. He was like a little furnace, and before she knew it she fell into a sound sleep. And for the first time since her mother was alive, she felt safe.

A SOFT ORANGE light illuminated the edges of the curtains. It was almost time. Oz had only slept an hour or so. He needed more, but he was always too wired before a battle. And he had no delusions. This would be a battle.

"You're up," Ronnie said from behind him.

He turned with a small smile, but it widened when the sheet slipped to reveal her bountiful breasts. They seemed to call to him, and he pounced. With grace, speed and agility, he was across the room and on top of her in two steps. He needed to taste her, kiss her, touch her.

He leaned in and kissed her neck and inhaled the scent that was uniquely Ronnie. He pulled away for just a moment to admire all of her curves and bask in her beauty. The top sheet pooled at her waist and he couldn't help but reach out for the luscious nipple that seemed to perk up the moment he looked at them. Ronnie fell back just out of reach. With her arms above her head, she looked like a goddess. One he was about to devour.

The door opened, and bright sunlight flooded the room. Ronnie gasped with wide eyes toward the open door. Oz's hand touched the bed and as quick as a snap, Ronnie appeared to be dressed, blocking out her actual nudity from the intruder.

"Don't move," Oz whispered to Ronnie. "You might flash him."

Ronnie nodded slowly, staring at the realistic clothes she now had on.

"You guys…" Kitty walked through the door, then froze, eyeing them suspiciously. "Ready to go?"

"Don't you knock?" Oz didn't move from the bed. When using his power in such a small space, like covering one person with clothes, it worked best when he didn't move too much.

"I'll wait outside." Kit slowly stepped back out of the room.

"Good idea."

Once the door closed, Oz moved his hand, and the illusion faded away.

"What did you just do?"

"As a shifter, some of us have special abilities. I can create illusions."

"That looked so real." She looked down at herself. "My clothes—"

"Yeah, an older lady brought these for you while you were sleeping." Oz grabbed the jeans and t-shirt and hoodie from the side chair. "Hurry up and get dressed, then we'll go over the game plan."

Ronnie slid off the bed with the bedsheet held in a tight fist over her breasts, then grabbed the clean clothes from him.

"Thanks," she said shyly, before hurrying off to the bathroom.

He'd seen all of her, but she wasn't quite ready to parade around in the buff in front of him just yet. But she would… soon enough.

About ten minutes later, the front door opened a little.

A fully dressed Ronnie pulled it open wider. "Come on in, Kit."

At the bed, Oz pulled his leather duster on over his cut. He opened the inside front and pulled out four six inch throwing knives from an inside band and slid them back. He checked both sides.

"What's the plan?" Kitty looked at Oz who was still pulling knives from every conceivable spot in his coat.

"What about the bus?"

"Six has Clutch driving the bus down. He should be here in two hours."

"Two hours! Shit, that's too late. This thing is about to go down now."

"I told you. I can handle that part," Ronnie chimed in.

Oz didn't like that she would hot-wire a truck from the parking lot, but they needed the wheels. Not being a hypocrite or anything, he just wanted his woman's hands to stay clean. Lord knows he's done some things he wasn't proud of that were far from legal.

"So?"

"Dammit, fine."

Ronnie gave him a tight smile. "I won't screw it up. I'll need five minutes when we're ready."

"What's happening?" Kitty looked between them.

Oz waved at Ronnie in a "You tell him" way.

"I'm going to borrow," she used air quotes, "a vehicle from the parking lot and I will return it before they know it's missing." Ronnie's smile beamed.

Kit lifted a brow and smiled in appreciation. "Nice."

"I'll ride with her, get her close and hide the truck. You can go the route we found earlier, then wait for my signal."

"What's going to be the signal?" Ronnie asked.

Oz smiled. "You won't miss it. I promise."

CHAPTER TWELVE

S now. Oz was right, Ronnie thought as she held her hand out to touch "the signal." It floated through her hand, but it looked like it melted. Ronnie and Oz ducked down when they reached the large compound. A stone grandiose mansion sat across from a snow covered clearing.

The lion's lair now looked more like a winter wonderland. Snow flurries floated down to the ground in slow succession. The natural crisp evening air helped to sell the illusion.

Oz and Ronnie had hidden the truck about two miles away and walked through the wooded area, creating a new path. There was one road in and out of the lion's compound, and they were nowhere near it. It wasn't a long walk, but it stank to high heaven. These men must not have running water or even heard of the word hygiene. She was human and she could smell them.

"Over there." Oz pointed to the cluster of rusted out railcars on the edge of the cleared property. "I'm sure they're holding the girls there. Once I open the doors, get the girls to the truck and haul ass."

"What about you guys?"

"We'll be fine. Just stick to the plan."

"The plan. Okay." Ronnie nodded. But she didn't like splitting up.

The snow picked up and started coming down in sheets. After a minute or two, she could no longer see the mansion. Ronnie lifted her hands in front of her face, and could barely see them.

Oz grabbed her upheld hand. "Let's go."

The two dashed across the open area toward the enclosures. Each railcar had a combination lock on them as big as her hand. She'd never seen one so large before. Didn't even know they came that big.

Oz wrapped his hand around the lock and twisted then pulled. The metal thinned and squealed before it snapped.

The tiger's roar echoed around them.

"Kitty's in trouble. Here." He took off his cut and long coat. "Wear this. I'll see you back at the room." He handed her both, then broke the other two locks. "Be careful." He pulled her in for a quick kiss.

Before she could protest or argue he was running and pulling off the last of his clothes and leaped into the air a man, then landed a pure white snow leopard. He blended seamlessly into the falling snow. If she hadn't known he was just standing there, she wouldn't have.

She shrugged on the coats and wrenched the first railcar door open. It was heavy and hard to move, but she got it. The smell hit her like a sledgehammer, but she held her breath and pushed on.

"Golden! Golden, you in here?" Ronnie screamed into the darkness.

Four filthy heads popped out.

One girl couldn't have been any older than ten, with huge hazel eyes. "Are you here to save us?"

"Yes." Ronnie opened her arms to help the girl out.

Once the four girls were out, Ronnie asked. "Anybody else inside?"

They all shook their heads.

"Okay. Stay together, we need to get every one." Ronnie led the small group to each container.

She opened the door, and the stench nearly knocked her down. This one reeked of death, she was sure of it. Ronnie covered her nose with her hand. She knew no-one was alive inside, but called out anyway. "Hello." Her greeting was met by silence.

She quickly moved to the last railcar. "Golden! You in there?"

"They took her." A tentative voice said from the darkness. "But she said you would come. Ronnie, you're Ronnie, right?" A dark-haired teenager came to the opening. "I'm Mia."

She didn't look as bad as some of the others, Ronnie thought. "Yeah, I'm Ronnie. Come on, we gotta get out of here."

One by one, six more girls and two young boys of five or six stepped out. Ronnie's heart clutched. She had to get these children out of there. One little boy cried and cried with his arms up.

"Shhhh. Don't cry. You're safe now."

"You shouldn't lie to the kid like that," a gravelly voice said from behind her.

The girls recoiled and gasped. More started crying. "Girls," Ronnie said. "Go to the first car and stand there. No one can see you if you hide there."

"Don't. He's gonna kill you," Mia said. The girl gripped the sleeve of the duster, shifting the knives.

"I'll be okay." She handed Mia the crying boy and moved her hand under her coat to the small of her back.

Over the snarls and gunfire, Ronnie could hear him walking up behind her. "She's right, you know. I am going to kill you."

Ronnie pushed the children away. "Mia, take the kids. Stay together and hide. I'll be okay."

The teen's eyes grew large as she pulled the children away. "Run!"

Ronnie turned around holding the gun out of sight. The guard was in black military fatigues, but he didn't seem to have a gun or a weapon. Not one that she could see, anyway.

"You don't have to do this. I just want the children."

"King wouldn't appreciate it if I just gave the lambs away." He moved his arms away from his body.

Just before he leaped at her, he did something with his hands. Ronnie couldn't tell if he grabbed a knife or what. She pulled her guns and fired four shots. The weight of the massive man hit her like a freight train, and something sharp dug into her lower back at the same time.

The kids screamed from somewhere behind her. She told them to run and hide, it didn't sound like they had.

Blood had soaked into her top from the hole in the man's head. She wasn't sure she'd even hit him, he'd moved so fast. Ronnie opened her mouth to let the children know she was okay, but nothing came out. She pulled her arm from between her and the dead man. It took three good tries, but she got the dead man off of her. Blood poured from a few small holes in his neck and chest. Four long canines protruded from his mouth.

"You're okay," a young girl's voice said from behind her.

"I thought I told you guys to run." She was something, alive but she wasn't entirely sure she was okay. Her entire body trembled from adrenaline. Never in her life did she ever think she would have to shoot someone, let alone kill anyone.

"We couldn't leave you," Mia said.

"Are you guys okay?" Ronnie asked once she got stable on her wobbly legs. When they all nodded, she said, "Stay together. Let's go this way."

Ronnie and the kids stood at the cusp of freedom when shots rang out. The kids screamed and ran further into the trees to hide. But fear and worry over Oz, Kit, and Golden left her rooted out in the open. The whiteout conditions made it difficult to see Oz and Kit, but the exit through the trees was clear. Then a scream rang out that she knew better than her own voice.

Golden.

UNDER THE COVER of snow flurries, Kitty had taken out a few guards before the lions even knew what had hit them. Before Oz had taken Ronnie to the hostages, he witnessed a lion reaching for a snowflake, then being yanked into the tree-line. The bushes rustled, then nothing.

It was difficult to have Ronnie here in enemy territory. It terrified him to the core when he had to leave her to help that damned tiger. All the firepower in the world wouldn't help if a sneaky ass lion caught her by surprise. They wouldn't kill her. No, they'd use her, then sell her. This needed to end now.

Two lions had Kit pinned down. Oz ran full throttle and sank his teeth into the scrawny lion atop the large tiger. The lion torqued his thin frame and aimed for Oz's underbelly. Oz had used this technique many times, but the only difference being, he was faster and better at it. Oz lifted his lower half, kicking his legs up higher as the lion's paw swiped and missed. They hit the ground just as Oz's leopard wrenched back in the opposite direction, snapping the lion's neck. He gave another shake for good measure, insuring the limp lion was dead.

The leopard and tiger looked around at the dead bodies of lions, and humans covered in snow. An eerie silence fell over the compound.

We need to end this, now.

The tiger chuffed and through the blinding snow, Oz and Kit stalked in the direction of the mansion. The doors burst outward, splinters flying everywhere. A scarred, shirtless, dark-haired man lowered his leg and stepped out on the porch.

The leopard and tiger stopped their approach.

"You dare come into my house!" The lion with a scar down one side of his face looked directly at Oz through the haze of whiteness.

King Leonidas.

A younger man with dark blonde hair who looked very much like King but dressed more like he belonged in Miami instead of Texas in his Versace-esque shirt, gold chains, and beige linen pants, followed him out onto the front porch.

A heavy pressure laid across Oz's leopard's back like a slab of concrete, causing his knees to buckle. None of the other lions had this type of power. It just poured off of this lion in waves.

"Your tricks only work on weaker minded lions." He waved his hand dispassionately.

"Who are you talking to, Dad?" a young man asked looking around bewildered. "There's no one out there."

It became too difficult to maintain the illusion with this much strain on his body. The blizzard faltered. Oz had seen the King of the Demon Lion Pride a few times before, but he didn't know the man wielded this kind of power.

"Did you come for her?" King snatched a nearly naked girl by her light brown hair from a man in all black tactical gear. He dragged her behind him as she twisted and struggled, hitting the man's hand down the front steps.

He's going to kill me. Oh, God. Oh, God.

Golden's distress invigorated him. Oz's joints cracked and his muscles throbbed as he pushed upward against the lion's power. With a full body flex, the snow leopard stood tall. Oz didn't wait for an invitation, he sprinted toward the two.

A crack of thunder sounded around them, then liquid fire burned through his hind leg. He tumbled ass over shoulders, then landed about six feet from King.

Golden's screams reverberated through him and pierced his mind. *What's happening to me? It burns!*

Hold on, Golden. Hold her in. Oz repeated.

"I can't," Golden screamed out loud.

Kit. How you doing? Oz turned his head to look at the crouching tiger.

He's strong, but not strong enough to hold me. I'm ready when you are. Just say the word. The big tiger's head nodded ever so slightly.

The stress of the entire situation must have been too much for Ronnie's sister. Her eyes widened as they sparkled into a rich amber gold with flecks of silver. This couldn't be happening at a worst time.

King pulled Golden up, inhaled her hair. "Not long now. I can't wait to taste her."

"Dad, you got her for me."

"Shut the fuck up, Santi," King growled out the name as he lifted his hand to hit the young man.

Oz eyed the cowering young man. This must be the infamous stalker boyfriend, Santiago.

Santiago flinched, then another wave of pressure spread out. Oz didn't falter this time, but King's son fell to his knees.

Tears poured from Golden's eyes. "Ronela!"

Oz swirled his head around to see Ronnie walking up with both guns drawn. Goddammit that woman never listened. They were going to have to have a long talk about her listening to her man. Not that he was yet, but he was working on it.

"Let my sister go!"

"Big sister's here." King licked his lips.

"That's the bitch who took Golden from me the last time," Santiago said with a little growl in his voice.

"I can see. She's tough, that's going to make it even better when I take her and break her." King threw the convulsing Golden to the ground next to his son.

Oz knew the moment King tossed Golden what was about to happen. *Kit, get the girl.*

King snatched his pants off and shifted into a massive brown beast. Even in this form, he was scarred, and his left eye had a long scratch over it. His roar thundered through the silence. Ronnie's eyes widened, but she didn't stop coming.

Oz wanted to yell at her to run, but he couldn't. The lion moved faster than he'd anticipated, and was nearly on top of Ronnie, before she got her first shot off.

Santiago burst through his clothes, reared at the oncoming tiger, then took off toward Ronnie.

King's cat was huge, but even more intimidating as he stood on his hind legs. Over six feet of muscled lion towered over Ronnie. The guns clicked after hitting him at least ten times. The lion roared and swatted his huge paw at her. Oz knocked her out of the way just in time, taking part of the blow across his back.

Oz growled and Ronnie seemed to understand as she backpedaled out of the way. Blood poured from King's stomach and chest as he circled Oz. The lion leaped, aiming for the smaller cat's neck, but Oz was agile and faster than the heavier cat. He twisted out of the reach of the gaping maw. After a few swipes, Oz maneuvered around the injured lion and when he reared to hit him, Oz went low using one long talon to open up the lion's stomach as if he'd used a scalpel.

Oz slid to a stop, kicking up dirt and gravel. King limped and pushed slowly to stand. A hurt lion is a dangerous lion. His heart thudded in his chest when he saw his woman sneaking up behind King. The lion must have been seriously hurt not to have heard her. He was going to have a serious conversation with his woman about her safety.

Bam! Bam!

The lion's back end dropped to the ground, then moments later the rest of him fell to the ground causing a plume of dust to kick up.

"Good." Ronnie looked up from the dead lion to him. "Geez, Oz, you're covered in blood. You hurt bad?"

Now was one of those times he wished he could tell her what was on his mind. He yelped when she touched his back leg.

Wizard, you are not going to believe this.

Oz didn't want to hear or see anything else. *Santiago?*

That little coward ran off after I hit him once.

"Oh, my God." Ronnie fell to her knees. "Golden is that you?"

A small pale white tiger with patches of gold stood behind the huge bengal tiger.

"Goldie, come out, baby," Ronnie coaxed. "I love you.

You hear me? I love you. I don't care what form you take. You are my little sister."

It's okay, Golden. Your sister knows all about you.

I don't even know all about me. The little tiger tentatively moved from behind Kit and nuzzled Ronnie.

I'll explain it when we get back. Oz nuzzled her too.

I didn't know there were any golden tigers left. Kit walked around the group.

Neither did I, Oz responded.

Ronnie kissed Golden's furry head, then looked around at the collection of big cats, then scanned the trees behind her. "I gotta get the kids out of here. Maybe the bus is at the motel by now. I'll see you guys back there." She kissed the tiger, then Oz. "I'm glad you didn't die."

Ronnie had a slight limp as she walked away. Surely she would have said something if she was hurt. He'd get her out of those clothes and cleaned up the moment they got back to the room.

CHAPTER THIRTEEN

Oz limped out of the trees that lined the back edge of the motel. The first thing he spotted was the large black Tahoe blocking three parking spots in the middle of the parking lot. Clutch leaned against the door, smoking a cigarette. Oz had just pulled on his t-shirt when he spotted Six, his president, sitting on his bike with his old lady, Twistie.

"Happy you guys made it down," Oz said as he walked up.

Six held out his hand and Oz clasped his president's outstretched arm below the elbow, and leaned into a half hug.

"You okay, brother?" Six lifted his head toward his legs.

Oz looked down. His thigh still hurt like hell from where the lion shot him. "Yeah, I had to dig out a bullet. It'll be fully healed in no time."

Six nodded.

Twistie smiled up at him. "I heard you found a baby tiger."

"Yeah. *Uncle* Kit is around here somewhere, explaining to her what we are. And doing tiger-type shit."

"Oz, you alright? You're fucking talking… out loud," Six stated as he patted his shoulder.

"Yeah, long story." Oz gave a nervous laugh.

Twistie and Six laughed with him.

"Babe, I'm going to go find those tigers." Twistie leaned in and Six lowered his mouth to kiss his mate.

Before, them kissing like this bothered Oz, even drove him to leave town for a few days. And thank God for these two being so damned amorous and having noisy sex. If he hadn't left, he would never have found Ronnie. Now, he knew what love felt like. Now, he understood what it meant to have a mate. Now, his soul was intertwined with a woman he would never let go of for anything.

Six slapped his woman's ass before she walked away. She looked back, winked, then put a little extra sway in her hips. He looked around the parking lot before lowering his voice. "Where are the girls?"

"Mostly girls, but some boys too. Ronnie should've gotten here already." Oz looked around as well.

A dark-haired teen wandered into the parking lot, crying his name. "Oz! Are you here? Oz!"

Oz and Six rushed towards the girl. "Whoa!" Oz held out his hand like he was calming a wild beast. "I'm Oz."

"Ms. Ronnie said to show you this." She held out his cut.

Oz lifted his leather club vest to see bloodstains on it.

Six whistled behind him. "Clutch, get the bus."

"What happened? Where is she?" Oz tried to keep a calm tone in his voice, but the girl flinched a couple of times, anyway.

"This way," she said and led him out to the main road.

"Are the rest of you okay? Was it an accident?" Oz wanted to run the next couple of miles until he found her. It took a lot for him to not leave the girl.

She jogged as she talked. "Is Golden okay? They took her and…" The girl got choked up.

Oz just wanted to find his woman. His stomach was turning cartwheels, and this girl kept going on. "Yes. She's okay."

"She said you guys would come," the teen continued, then pointed. "Ms. Ronnie's there."

Oz had already spotted the parked truck on the side of the road and took off running.

"Ronnie?" Oz nearly pulled the door off its hinges when he opened it.

Her dark skin now had a mottled gray cast. What the fuck happened in the last thirty minutes?

Her head kind of rocked and fell when she looked at him. "Oz," she whispered. "You're here."

"What happened? You were fine when you left."

"I'm not sure. But I can't feel my legs."

He didn't see anything right off. His fingers tentatively touched a trail up her leg and she didn't react, but then he saw it. Pools and pools of red had soaked through his long coat and soaked into the driver's side seat.

"Baby, this might hurt. Forgive me." Oz pushed her torso forward and opened the coat and preceded to lift her shirt.

She hissed out her discomfort, and he slowed down. "Sorry. Sorry. I just need a quick peek."

Shit! He could see exactly what it was. She didn't get shot. The two four-inch gashes oozed blood and the smell of poison rankled his nose. She must've been losing pints the entire time and didn't know it. Adrenaline and purpose will do that.

"Is Golden alright?" Ronnie said after he leaned her back into place.

"Yeah. She's fine."

Six, get the kids out of here. Now.

Already on it, brother.

"Is she going to be okay?" The teen asked from behind him.

He took two deep breaths before turning to answer. "Yes. We'll take good care of her. Thank you. Now, go with my brothers." He pointed toward the black vehicle where the kids were loading up. "They will get you guys back home."

"Thank you. I don't know what would've happened if..." Tears filled the teenager's eyes as she gave him a curt nod before running toward the club's SUV.

Oz stepped away from the truck. The bus rolled past him, then Six and Kitty walked up.

"What can we do?" Six grabbed him by the shoulders.

Oz kept shaking his head. "I don't know. She's lost a lot of blood and humans don't heal like we do. She doesn't smell right. I think they poisoned her."

"Number one, we gotta get her off the highway. I assume that's stolen." Six pointed to the truck.

"Borrowed." Oz repeated Ronnie's words.

"Fine." Six said, then turned to Kitty stating, "When we take her inside, clean it and dump it somewhere."

"Somewhere they can find it. Ronnie wanted them to have it back," Oz added.

"Done. Clean it up as best as you can, leave some money for repairs."

Oz felt drugged. His limbs moved liked boulders, and his legs were stuck in mud. When he and the others made it back to the vehicle, Ronnie didn't move.

"You want me to..." Six put his arms out as if to take her.

"No, I got it." Oz wiped his face before reaching for her. There weren't any tears, but he wanted to cry.

Ronnie slid into his arms. A perfect fit. He wasn't giving

up on this woman. She fought fucking shifters with him, no other female he knew had this much courage. She was his, and he would fight for her.

He ran faster than he'd ever ran before, all while not trying to jostle her too much.

Kitty, where's Golden?

In my room.

Good.

Six opened the motel room door, and Oz laid Ronnie down. He placed her on her stomach instead of her back, where the injuries were, then pulled out a knife.

"Yo, yo what're you doing?" Six held Oz's knife hand.

"All of her injuries are on her back. Go grab some towels and I'll need a first aid kit. If I can stop the bleeding and get her conscious, then maybe I can change her so she can heal herself."

"She's weak, man. That's seriously risky."

"What do you want me to do? Watch her die?"

Six released his hand and Oz sliced open his favorite leather duster from neck to hem. She wouldn't die. Not on his watch.

After using every towel in the motel, using all the alcohol swabs and bandages from every first aid kit they could find, and destroying a mattress; Ronnie was steadily slipping away before his eyes.

Six patted his shoulder. "I'm sorry."

Oz didn't want their sorries; he wanted his mate. In such a short amount of time, Ronnie meant everything to him. He pulled her into his embrace, and the taint of the poison was ruining her scent. Smelling this made him want to kill those lions all over again.

With his eyes closed, he kissed her on the lips. No response.

On the cheek. No response.

On the neck. Not a flinch.

"I've waited me entire life for you. You're my mate. Ronela Garrison, you hear me? I love you and I won't lose you." His leopard came to the surface. Instead of changing completely, only his canines elongated, then he struck. Biting her fast and hard on the shoulder.

ONE WEEK. Oz had been waiting one week for Ronnie to wake up. Anxiety wracked him as he considered what would happen when Ronnie found out he bit her without her permission. The thought of her not being in this world was a worse fate than her not forgiving him. But seeing her in his bed had been a gift that he prayed wouldn't ever end.

Golden was still in tiger form as she laid next to her sister. Oz sat on the other side of the bed, holding her hand with his head down.

"Hey," Ronnie said in a raspier voice than her normal tone.

Oz's head popped up. "You're awake."

She shifted to raise up, using her arms to push up. "Ow, ow, ow."

Oz's hands flew out to help her. "Go slow."

Her thigh bumped against the small tiger in the bed. "Ouch." She moved slower, then rested against the headboard. "Wow. Is that…?"

"Yep, that's your baby sister."

Golden's head popped up. Ronnie sank her fingers into the little tiger's soft fur.

"My mom always said you were special, I never thought

you'd be rare too." She scratched her behind the ears. "Why is she still a tiger?"

"The first turn is always the hardest and being stressed hasn't helped. It may take her a few more days before she can turn back."

Ronnie looked around the room. "Where are we? This isn't the motel."

"It's my place. After you were stable, I brought you to San Antonio. I hope that's all right?"

"Yeah." She nodded in approval. "It's a nice place, thank you. Oz, tell me what happened. I remember driving the girls... Oh, my God! Are the kids okay? Did I crash?"

"No, Baby-girl, calm down. Almost all of the kids are back home, now."

Ronnie brow creased. "How long have I been out?"

"About a week."

"Tell me exactly what happened."

"We're pretty sure the guy who stabbed you had an anti-coagulant on his blades. So, the cut wasn't deep, but you just kept bleeding."

"Jesus, I could have died. I feel good now - a little sore. Who do I have to thank?" Ronnie asked with a huge smile.

She was killing him. He patted her hand.

Golden, could you give us a minute?

No. I want to hear it. I know what you did. I can smell it on her.

Oz didn't roll his eyes, but he wanted to. "Ronnie, in order to save you I had to do something. Something... I, um."

Ronnie squeezed his hand. "Just say it. It can't be that bad."

"In order to save your life I had to bite you... convert you."

Ronnie's eyes went wide. "Into what?"

The small tiger jumped off the bed. Through a host of growls and grunts, the small tiger's back bowed as the white and golden hair rippled away.

Ronnie pushed up to see. "What's happening to her?"

"Looks like she's changing back." Oz grabbed the blanket from the end of the bed and held it wide. A very naked Golden grabbed the corners and tucked it tightly around her, like a strapless dress.

"Damn that hurt." Golden rolled her shoulders. "Ronnie. He bit you to save you. You're one of us now." Golden grabbed Ronnie's hand.

"I'm a tiger?" Ronnie looked between Golden and Oz.

"No." Golden reached out behind her and Oz took her hand. "Tell her." She pulled him closer.

"To save you, I made you a shifter."

"You made me a... leopard." Ronnie said slowly. "A snow leopard... like you?"

Oz nodded, then waited with bated breath on how she was going to take this. He'd decided to leave the mate part out until later.

"Please don't be mad, Ronela."

"Yeah, Ronela," Oz said with a hopeful smile.

Ronnie lifted one brow. "Don't you dare."

Oz lifted his hands in surrender.

"I'm not mad. I'm taking it all in. I'm alive and a big cat, now."

"So, we can stay. Kit said he'd teach me all about being a tiger."

"That's kind of scary, but tigers are my favorite."

Oz growled. "Woman, I'm standing right here."

The girls laughed.

"But there's this one snow leopard I know who is cool, gorgeous, and pretty damned awesome." Ronnie stared at Oz, then lifted a brow. "Goldie, can you excuse us, please?"

Golden leaned in and whispered, "Be nice to him." Then kissed her on the cheek. "I love you."

"I love you too, kid," Ronnie said as Golden jumped off the bed.

Golden stopped next to Oz's shoulder. "Remember what I told you when we first met. Now would be a good time." She winked, then left the room.

Oz stepped closer. Ronnie patted the spot beside her, and he sat down. "What was that about?"

"I'll tell you in a minute." Oz touched her cheek and got lost in her eyes.

"I want to thank you for saving Golden," Ronnie said as she touched his fingers. "And me."

"I was happy to do it. We saved so many lives." Oz intertwined his fingers in hers and laid them in her lap.

"You're a great man, Oz Zhang."

He began to shake his head before she finished. "Not really."

"I think so. Now tell me. What did my sister say to you? Something embarrassing, I bet."

He pulled her into his arms and kissed her deeply. It actually made his toes curl, but he wasn't going to tell her that. When they pulled apart, he pressed his forehead to hers.

"She told me you hadn't been properly kissed in a really long while."

"That brat!"

"I'm beginning to see that." Oz smiled.

"Hey, Oz."

He murmured something like a, "Hmmm," as he nuzzled her neck.

"I'm your mate, huh?"

THE END

May Day - A Gray Witch Novel

Day of the Dead - Gray Witch #2

ABOUT THE AUTHOR

R.R. Born lives in Houston, TX with her husband and an orange tabby terror named Pele. She has a degree in Photography from Houston Community College and a BA in Film/Screenwriting from Long Island University in Brookville, NY. She's worked as a Production Coordinator, Second Assistant Director on local commercials, TLC & HGTV shows, and movies.

 facebook.com/rrborn16

 twitter.com/rrborn16

 instagram.com/rrborn_author